# BURDEN OF
# HONOR

# Between Two Flags

# An American Adventure

# BURDEN OF HONOR

# LEE RODDY

**BETHANY HOUSE PUBLISHERS**
MINNEAPOLIS, MINNESOTA 55438

*Burden of Honor*
Copyright © 1999
Lee Roddy

Cover illustration by Chris Ellison
Cover design by the Lookout Design Group

Published by Bethany House Publishers
A Ministry of Bethany Fellowship International
11400 Hampshire Avenue South
Minneapolis, Minnesota 55438
www.bethanyhouse.com

Printed in the United States of America by
Bethany Press International, Minneapolis, Minnesota 55438

Library of Congress Cataloging-in-Publication Data

CIP data applied for

ISBN 0-7642-2027-6                                        CIP

To my eleven-year-old grandsons,
Patrick O'Shaughnessy Roddy
and
Zachary Steven de Haas

LEE RODDY is the award-winning and best-selling author of many books, television programs, and motion pictures, including *Grizzly Adams, Jesus,* and THE D. J. DILLION ADVENTURE SERIES, BHP's AN AMERICAN ADVENTURE, and THE LADD FAMILY SERIES with Focus on the Family. He and his wife make their home in California.

# CONTENTS

# PROLOGUE

*From Gideon Tugwell's journal, October 13, 1933*

Growing up is always hard, but it seemed especially so in the American Civil War of 1861–65 when I was a boy.

Looking back through the faded pages of my journal written in the second year of that bloody conflict, I again feel the agony of uncertainty my friends and I experienced.

It wasn't just my own growing-up pains that I remember but those of two other special people who were part of my life back then.

There was Emily, the Yankee girl unwillingly trapped in the Confederacy when the war started. She almost made history in a way she never wanted.

There was also Nat, a runaway slave boy, who had reached freedom in Canada only to risk his precious liberty and return. He tried to do what few black people ever could after their families were sold apart.

I also had my share of troubles in that war-ravaged spring and early summer of 1862. Time has dulled the pain, but not the memories.

The invading Yankees seemed about to seize Richmond, Virginia, the capital of the Confederacy at that time. That was the last place Emily, Nat, or I wanted to be, but that's where we all ended up during the climactic conflict now known as the Seven Day's Campaign.

This is the way it happened, more than seventy years ago.

★ ★

# STRANGER AT A GRAVE

*April, 1862*

He told himself that he was too old to cry, but the tears seeped through his tightly closed eyelids as he knelt beside the settling mound. He pounded it with his fists and whispered in great anguish, "Why, Papa? Why did you die and leave us with all this mess? Why? Why?"

Instantly conscience-stricken, Gideon moaned in grief and threw himself facedown across the grave. "I'm sorry, Papa! I know you didn't want to die. But I've tried so hard, yet we're going to . . . to lose everything because . . . " his voice quivered, and he finished in a broken sob, "because I can't do what you did, and I don't know what to do now!"

Painful sobs choked off his words, and Gideon let the hurt, anger, and frustration grip his slender but wiry body. He was unmindful of the fresh, clean smell of early spring, the first green leaves on the trees, and the low hum of bees.

Tired, discouraged, and alone, Gideon ignored the cold dampness of the earth beneath his frayed, homespun clothes. He was not aware of anything except his own agony while he cried himself out at the small Tugwell family cemetery. It was fenced off in a corner of the hardscrabble farm near Church Creek, Virginia.

After a while, Gideon slowly raised his head and looked

★ ★

11

through misty blue eyes at the brilliant morning sky. "Tell Papa I'm sorry, Lord," he murmured. "I didn't mean those awful things. I—" He broke off at the flash of red as a cardinal landed on a nearby branch. It cocked its plumed head to study the prone boy, then broke into song.

"I know," Gideon said softly to the bird. "It's spring, and you're happy. I wish I—"

He interrupted himself when the bird suddenly gave a cry of alarm and flew away. Gideon heard footsteps behind him and raised himself from the grave to look over his shoulder.

A stranger in a frayed Confederate infantry uniform staggered toward him. Embarrassed at being caught in his tears, Gideon wiped a callused hand across his eyes and lashed out in anger. "Who are you? What're you doing on our property? Hey! You're drunk, and it's not even noon!"

"No, I'm not . . ." the man said before his knees buckled and he slowly collapsed. He thrust out both hands to break his fall.

Thirteen-year-old Gideon quickly rolled away as the man sprawled across the grave. The boy leaped to his feet, staring down at the stranger. He moaned softly, his eyes closed. That's when Gideon saw that the stranger's left hand was missing.

"What's the matter, mister?" he asked, kneeling. There was no answer. Gideon gingerly placed his hand on the man's flushed cheek. "You're burning up!" he exclaimed.

For a moment, the boy stared uncertainly at the silent figure before him. Then Gideon quickly turned around and ran across the field toward home.

His mother, younger brother, two sisters, and both family hounds followed Gideon back to where the victim still lay as he had fallen. Mrs. Tugwell briefly examined him, then motioned the girls away. "He might be contagious, so you two stay back. Gideon, you and Ben have had about all the sicknesses, so you can help me."

Kate took Lilly's hand and backed away, asking their mother, "What's wrong with him, Mama?"

★ ★

"I don't know yet. Fever could mean several things," she replied, "but we've got to bring it down as fast as possible. Let's get him into the house and apply cold compresses. Gideon, hitch Hercules to the sledge so we can move him."

Eleven-year-old Ben said, "The wagon would be faster."

His mother shook her head, the loose strands of dark hair trailing across her furrowed brow. "We could never lift him that high. Now, help your brother, and hurry."

The boys soon returned, both standing on the low, strong sledge, which was commonly used for carrying heavy logs. Gideon held the reins that guided the big mule back to the graveyard.

It was a struggle for mother and sons to push, pull, and roll the unconscious man onto the flat sledge. All the while, the family spoke in subdued tones, except when Gideon ordered the two hounds away from sniffing suspiciously at the stranger.

Hercules easily pulled the sledge and all the people to the back porch of the Tugwells' small house. Mrs. Tugwell told the girls to draw fresh water from the well while the boys helped get the man off the sledge.

The efforts roused him enough to weakly stand, then stagger inside, leaning on Gideon and his mother. They put him into the boys' tiny bedroom, struggling to guide him through the narrow space between the three built-in pole bunks and the handmade chest of drawers. They eased him into the lower bunk, where Isham, Gideon's older half brother, had slept before he went off to fight the Yankees almost a year ago.

With cool water, Mrs. Tugwell repeatedly applied cold compresses to the stranger's fevered brow. At his mother's instruction, Gideon searched the man's pockets for identification, but there wasn't any. When he seemed asleep, she closed the bedroom door and gathered the children around her in the kitchen.

Gideon slid onto the homemade bench beside Ben. Kate, who would turn seven in a few days, and Lilly, who was just

★ ★

five the month before, joined their mother on the bench on the other side of the sawbuck table. All four children looked expectantly at their mother.

Wide-eyed little Lilly asked, "Is he going to die like Papa?"

"I hope not." Mrs. Tugwell put her arm around the youngest child and drew her close. "But we must all be quiet so he can rest."

Ben brushed uncombed brown hair away from his eyes. "What happened to his hand, Mama?"

"Lost in the war, most likely. He's still wearing his uniform. From the looks of his wrist, I'd guess it happened months ago. Maybe even last July during the battle at Manassas."

"Where Isham was wounded," Kate added.

Mrs. Tugwell nodded. Her then eighteen-year-old stepson had been hit in the arm while repelling the invading Union soldiers at a creek called Bull Run. The Confederates named the battle for the nearby railroad junction known as Manassas. Isham had recovered and returned to duty.

Their mother continued. "I imagine they discharged this stranger when his hand was healed enough. He was probably heading for his home when he got sick and turned in here."

Shaking his head, Gideon declared, "We're too far out of the way, Mama. Was it possible he was coming here, maybe with a message from Isham?"

"I suppose that's possible." She absently moved the coal-oil lamp aside so there would be no obstruction between her and the boys. "I wish we knew his name so we could notify his family. I don't know why the army doesn't make each soldier carry some kind of identification."

Gideon nodded as he remembered Isham saying that some men wrote their name on a piece of paper and put it in their pocket before a battle so they could be identified if killed in action.

Mrs. Tugwell leaned toward Gideon to ask, "Are you all right?"

★ ★

"I'm fine," he replied shortly, turning his head away. He was ashamed of his outburst at his father's grave and quickly changed the subject. "What about him?" he asked, jerking his head toward the bedroom where the stranger lay.

"I was coming to that," Mrs. Tugwell replied. "Whoever he is, we've got to help him, but he needs more than we can give. We'd better call Dr. Janssen."

The boy looked at his mother to make sure he had understood correctly. A doctor for a stranger? The family had barely had enough money for old Doc Janssen when Papa suffered his fatal heart attack last August.

Mrs. Tugwell seemed to read Gideon's mind. "It's got to be done, so we'll manage somehow. Maybe trade some setting hens for the doctor's services. If he does have a message from Isham, it's very important he gets well enough to tell us. Gideon, you'd better take Hercules and go fetch the doctor."

Gideon hurried outside and stood on the sledge while the mule pulled it around behind the barn. Both hounds trotted alongside. Gideon didn't waste time saddling Hercules; he simply unhitched him and swung onto his bare back, thumped him lightly with his heels just as the hounds suddenly broke into deep-voiced bawls, and raced into the wide, dusty yard. Gideon rode around the side of the barn, then groaned.

"Oh no! Not again!"

A fancy four-wheeled town coach rattled up the dusty, rutted drive. A pair of matched bays was driven by a gray-haired slave. He sat on the high outside seat, proudly wearing a red hat and bright green livery with gold buttons on a swallowtail coat.

Gideon's siblings rushed out of the back door to see why the hounds were barking. Ben took one look, then yelled toward the open kitchen window, "Mama! It's William Lodge again!"

Gideon glumly watched the coachman expertly turn the gold-striped black carriage so that the Briarstone Plantation crest glistened on the door. The driver pulled back on the reins, bringing the horses to a stop in their red shafts. The sunlight reflected off the team's black manes and tails as "Uncle" George stiffly climbed down and opened the door.

Gideon stopped the mule even with the carriage as William Lodge stepped haughtily to the ground. His quality clothes were in sharp contrast to the shabby garments Gideon wore.

William's father, a wealthy tobacco planter who owned nearby Briarstone Plantation, was off fighting the Union invaders. In his absence, his solidly built sixteen-year-old son was acting master of the plantation. He was every bit as hardheaded as his father. Both wanted to own the Tugwells' small but choice bottom farmland, which adjoined the large Briarstone tobacco plantation.

"Morning, Gideon," William said cordially. "Your mother home?"

Mrs. Tugwell was usually home except on the Sabbath when the family went to church. Gideon knew William was aware of that, so his remark was mere formality. What surprised Gideon was the visitor's pleasant tone. Most of the time he was contemptuous and had frequently threatened Gideon and even punched him.

Mrs. Tugwell stepped out onto the back porch, wiping her hands on a homemade apron. She eyed William with the same misgivings that Gideon felt. "William," she greeted him softly and briefly, stopping at the top step.

"You know why I'm here," William told her, standing by the carriage door.

Gideon was proud of his mother for ignoring William's obvious effort to force her to come to him, thereby asserting his superior social rank.

"I know," she admitted in the same soft tone.

"Under the law," the visitor began a bit pompously, "a woman cannot own property in her own name, but a widow has a one-third share so she can live on the property for the rest of her life. The oldest son inherits—"

"I know the law," Mrs. Tugwell interrupted, her voice hardening slightly. "You know from your previous visits that my stepson and I have written back and forth about this, and he doesn't want to sell."

"Yes, I'm aware of that, Mrs. Tugwell, but I've been watching this property since your husband died, and it's obvious that a mere boy"—William glanced disdainfully at Gideon—"can't do a man's work. Taxes will soon fall due, and you won't be able to pay them. You'll lose everything."

"No!" Gideon cried angrily, sliding off the mule's back and advancing toward William. "We will not!"

"Don't be a fool!" William snapped, spreading his feet and setting them solidly in the dust as if ready to engage in another fist fight. His polite veneer vanished. He warned, "I've beat up on you many times, but I'd hate to bloody your nose in front of your mother!"

Gideon stalked forward, his fists clenched. "I've gained some weight since the last time!"

His mother spoke firmly. "That's enough, son!"

Gideon stopped, teetering on the balls of his feet, struggling to control his stubborn urge to physically drive William and his threats away.

"William, I'd be obliged if you left my land at once!" Mrs. Tugwell said sharply.

He glared at her. "I'll go, but mark my words: There is no way you can farm this land by yourselves. When you lose it to taxes in the next few months, I'll get it!"

It took all of Gideon's willpower not to rush after William as he entered the coach.

When he was seated, William stuck his head out of the window. "Maybe it'll be sooner than that if the Yankee invaders hit you first!"

The old reinsman lightly snapped the lines over the matched team's backs, and the carriage began to move. William mouthed something that Gideon couldn't hear, but he knew what it was. William had said it often enough before: *"You're nothing but a white trash dirt farmer who will never amount to anything!"*

Gideon gritted his teeth but silently repeated his own vow: *We may be poor, but we're not trash! Someday I'm going to be somebody, and so will my family!*

The hounds bawled loudly and chased through the dust raised by the departing carriage. Gideon watched in frustration. It wasn't that he really wanted to keep the land; he hated farming and always had. It was wearing him down physically and emotionally, especially in the eight months since his father's fatal heart attack.

If it were up to Gideon, he would urge Isham to sell the land. Gideon longed to live in Richmond someday and become a book writer. But the farm was the only way the Tugwells had of scratching out a bare living.

Gideon was also held to the farm by his late father's determination never to sell or be run out by the greedy Lodges. Even if the family had another means of livelihood, they certainly could not, in good conscience, sell the land to the Lodges. But if taxes of forty cents and a hundred dollars' valuation weren't paid on time . . .

Gideon's mother's voice broke into his thoughts. "The doctor."

The boy nodded and returned to the mule, but his mind was not on the sick man so much as it was on the terrible problem that William presented.

It was hard for Gideon to understand how a miserable human being like William could be a cousin to orphaned Emily Lodge. She was only a few months younger than Gideon and was about the only person with whom he felt comfortable sharing his thoughts and feelings.

She had promised to write after leaving Briarstone last

★ ★

summer for the Confederate capital at Richmond, but he hadn't heard a word from her.

"Can't think about that now," he muttered. There were more immediate and pressing concerns. Gideon headed toward the village, urging the mule to a faster pace.

★ ★

# SECRETS AND LETTERS

Things were not going well with Emily Lodge. She sighed, lifted her long, full skirt above her shoes, and wearily climbed the half dozen stairs to the small front porch of Mrs. Lydia Stonum's two-story frame house. The pretty blond girl blinked violet eyes still misted with tears from her latest disappointment.

She inserted the skeleton key into the lock, then stopped and looked back. More Confederate troops marched down the street singing "Dixie." Emily wondered how they could do that after the terrible losses at Shiloh Church in Tennessee. North and South had suffered almost twenty-four thousand casualties in the two-day battle. That was more than in all previous American wars combined.

Entering the house, she removed her bonnet and tried to smile in greeting the forty-three-year-old widow, who had given her food and lodging for the past eight months.

Mrs. Stonum looked up from where she was sewing by the nearest window. "I can see it in your face," she said softly. "More bad news?"

Emily nodded, hanging her cloak and bonnet on the rack by the front door. "The provost marshal still won't give me a pass. It's so discouraging." The provost marshal was the army commander's officer in charge of military police. His power now extended to include civilians because Richmond was under martial law.

Mrs. Stonum's flying fingers stopped. She was a slender woman with dark hair parted in the middle and pulled back, which was the current style. She asked, "What excuse did they give this time?"

Emily dropped wearily into a heavy chair opposite her. In sharp contrast to the older woman's severe appearance, the thirteen-year-old defied the current hairstyle by rolling hers over a cushion in front. She did not part her hair in the middle, but allowed long golden sausage curls to cascade down the back of her neck to touch her shoulders.

"No excuse," she replied, pursing her small mouth. "They just asked ridiculous questions such as, 'Since you're a Yankee, Miss Lodge, do you have any relatives in the Union army or navy?'" Emily shook her head. "Mrs. Stonum, I've told them many times before that my only living relatives are Uncle Silas Lodge and his family at Church Creek here in Virginia. The provost marshal's people speak highly of Uncle Silas, but those officers just don't want to give me a pass back to Illinois! They act as if I'm a spy or something!"

"Maybe you should forget about it and stay on with us. After all, your parents and siblings are dead, and there are no other relatives living there. Except for your best girl friend, there's nobody left—"

"No!" Emily broke in. "I'm sorry to sound rude, but I've got to go back, even if only Jessie Barlow remains!" Emily paused, briefly thinking of Jessie's older brother, Brice, who was a Union cavalryman. She pushed the thought aside and rushed on. "Besides, I can't go on living here without paying you! Helping clean the house, doing the laundry, and washing dishes won't really pay for the food I eat, not to mention the room you let me share with Hannah! I'm going to have to find work if I don't get that pass!"

"You also help me with nursing sick people, Emily. I don't

want you to apply at the munitions factory where Hannah works. You have a different temperament—"

A knock at the door interrupted their conversation. Emily opened it to a slender man in his midthirties wearing a long coat. "Emily?" he asked, leaning toward her. "Emily Lodge! Is that you?"

It took her a second to recognize him. "Oliver Fitzhugh!" she exclaimed. "I haven't seen you since I lived at Briarstone! What brings you to Richmond?"

"Well, the army wouldn't take me because of a health problem, and since the Confederate mail service isn't too dependable, I'm delivering mail for a fee. I have a prepaid letter for Mrs. Lydia Stonum—"

"She's right here!" Emily interrupted, opening the door and motioning for Fitzhugh to enter. "Let me take your coat."

The widow briefly acknowledged Emily's introduction to the former Temperance speaker, then apprehensively took the letter. Emily suspected Mrs. Stonum thought it might be more bad news, but after reading a few lines, she smiled in relief.

"Mr. Fitzhugh," she said, "this requires a prompt response. Do you have a moment while I write one?"

"Of course," he said heartily. "It'll give Emily and me a chance to catch up on the news about old friends."

As Mrs. Stonum hurried upstairs, Emily and Fitzhugh spoke briefly about the war and her struggle to obtain a pass through Confederate lines.

Fitzhugh clucked his tongue in sympathy. "You think that's simply because you're a Yankee?"

"I'm positive! They say there are spies everywhere, and they seem to think I'm one of them! But it wasn't my idea to come live here in the South! If my family had lived—" She broke off and bit her lower lip to keep it from trembling.

"I'm sorry, Emily. I truly am."

She gained control of her emotions. "Thank you."

★ ★

"Perhaps you'd like to hear about your relatives at Briarstone."

"Yes, I would. Especially Julie." She added silently, *And my friend Gideon, too.*

"Your uncle Silas is still away with the cavalry troop he formed," Fitzhugh began. "As usual, your aunt is not well, but your cousin William manages the plantation quite nicely. He's still furious because his body servant ran away with the help of the Underground Railroad."

Emily licked her lips. Nat, the fugitive slave boy, had been hidden in a false compartment of the same wagon she had ridden boldly from Briarstone to Richmond last year.

"Your cousin Julie," Fitzhugh continued, "has become a fair hand at cooking even though there are black folks to do such menial things. That's because your uncle feels Julie should be prepared if the Yankees invade Briarstone and everyone is forced to become refugees."

He droned on, but Emily barely heard him. She had too many unpleasant memories of her aunt and William ordering her to leave Briarstone because of her strong Union comments. She wanted to ask about Gideon, but Fitzhugh shifted the conversation to Mrs. Stonum.

"I've heard," he began, "that she's a widow."

"Sadly true," Emily replied. "Her husband was a major who died in the Shenandoah Valley fighting beside General Stonewall Jackson. She lost one son at Manassas, and another on picket duty was killed by a sharpshooter."

"How sad! How very, very sad!"

Emily nodded. "The surgeons are all in the army, so Mrs. Stonum also helps local folks who need a doctor. I've gone with her to help where I can. Lately, she's been nursing at local military hospitals, too."

Fitzhugh's eyebrows shot up. "Really?" At Emily's nod, he asked casually, "Do you ever help her there?"

She gave Fitzhugh a wry smile. "Surgeons don't like girls

★ ★

around the hospital tents or buildings. But they let me read to the wounded, talk, or write letters for those who can't do it themselves. Things like that."

"I see." Fitzhugh pursed thin lips and fell silent.

"Gideon Tugwell," Emily said suddenly. "How's he doing since his father died? I mean . . . how's the family doing?"

"I haven't seen any of them, but William is trying hard to buy the Tugwells' prime piece of bottomland."

That didn't surprise Emily. "I've written Gideon some letters but never mailed them. I haven't heard from him, either."

Fitzhugh's eyes narrowed thoughtfully. "If it's a matter of shortage of funds, perhaps I have a solution."

Emily's heart leaped in hope. "Oh?"

After a quick glance toward the stairs, Fitzhugh leaned to Emily and lowered his voice. "Yes. You see, people expect me to know about everything because I travel among various towns and villages. If you will help me keep abreast of what you see and hear around Richmond, especially from wounded soldiers, I will deliver your letters for free."

"You will?" Emily impulsively reached out and gripped his hand. "Oh, Mr. Fitzhugh! Thank you!"

"You're welcome." He again glanced at the stairs before adding, "Naturally, it wouldn't be fair to do this for you and not Mrs. Stonum or others, so this must be our little secret. Fair enough?"

She nodded, too excited to say more.

Fitzhugh kept his voice low. "Tell me now what I might share with others on my rounds. Before I leave, you can quietly slip a couple of your letters to Gideon into my coat pocket."

After he left with Mrs. Stonum's letter and two of her own, Emily stood pensively at the front window watching Fitzhugh walk toward a light two-wheeled gig parked at the curb. A young black boy held the horse's reins.

Emily had an uneasy feeling about hiding anything from Mrs. Stonum; she was doing Emily a favor. But Fitzhugh had set his secret terms, and Emily honored them.

The slave deposited into his pocket Mrs. Stonum's Confederate paper "shinplaster"—the Confederacy's beleaguered currency—which Fitzhugh had casually pressed into his hand. Emily's thoughts jumped back to Nat. *I hope he reached freedom safely.*

★　★　★　★　★

Nat stopped currying the Quaker's big draft horse. He forgot the Canadian chill in the barn and took a step closer to a newly arrived fugitive slave. "My mother and little sister? Are you sure, Byrl?" he asked excitedly.

"Sho' I'se sho'!" Byrl and sixteen-year-old Nat had been slaves at Glenbury Hill in Virginia before Thaddaeus Whitman died and his heirs sold them to pay bills. Now in his fifties, Byrl still spoke in slave dialect, claiming he was too old to learn to read and write or speak proper English. In violation of the law, the mistress at Glenbury had taught Nat and other family slaves to do these things.

Nat felt hope surging through him. He hadn't heard a word since his mother, three younger brothers, and little sister had been sold separately a year ago.

"De same," Byrl continued, teeth flashing white with a pleased grin. "Seed dem bof' manys de time in dat bluebelly camp on de pin'sla. Yo' mammy was washin' de Yankee dogs clothes whilst de li'l sistah he'p—"

"Which peninsula camp?" Nat interrupted, stepping closer to the older man, who had arrived only the day before. "And when was the last time you saw them?"

"Lemme see, now." Byrl scratched his wooly dark hair, heavily streaked with gray. "Dem white Unnergroun' Rail folks move me plenty, most times at night, gittin' me to heah so I'se kin die free—"

Nat impatiently broke in. "A month ago? More? Less?"

Byrl refused to be hurried. "I'se studyin' on it."

★　★

Nat's excitement made him want to grab the older man by his bony shoulders and shake him. But that would have been useless. Whitman had been a benevolent master and had tolerated Byrl's habitual case of "the slows."

While the old runaway muttered to himself, figuring days when he had no knowledge of calendars, Nat reflected on what he had just been told. His mother, Lucy, age thirty-one, sister, Cordelia, age seven, and Byrl had recently been slaves on a peninsula plantation. They had escaped when the master and his family fled ahead of about one hundred thousand Yankees advancing up the peninsula. They planned to seize the Confederate capital and end the war. From the day they had been sold, Nat had set the seemingly impossible goal to find and lead all members of his family to freedom. That dream had kept him going after he was bought by William Lodge to serve as a body servant at Briarstone Plantation. Nat had run away after William gave him his first whipping.

It had taken a long time for daring "conductors" of the secret Underground Railroad to move Nat from Virginia through the Northern states and across the Canadian border to freedom. In the States, the Fugitive Slave Act required anyone to capture and return a fugitive slave to his master or face a thousand-dollar fine.

Finally Byrl decided. "Musta been 'bout thirty days ago. . . ." With prolonged pauses in between sentences, he gave the teen the information he needed.

Nat listened attentively, filling in the background from his own reading of newspapers. Last May, Union troops had invaded Virginia at two locations. One command crossed the Potomac from Washington and occupied the towns of Alexandria and Fairfax.

The second invasion force under General Ben Butler had sailed down the coast and landed at Fort Monroe on Virginia's peninsula between the York and James Rivers. Butler headed for Richmond. When three fugitive slaves entered his lines, he refused to return them to their owners, claiming them as "contraband of war."

As such, they were enemy property to be seized like crops or livestock. In 1857, the U.S. Supreme Court had ruled that a slave was property. Designating a fugitive slave as "contraband" was the Union army's way to bypass the Fugitive Slave Act. As contraband of war, slaves were put to work for the Yankees.

After Butler's failure on the peninsula, he had been replaced by General George McClellan. His massive forces were now trying to break the Confederate lines at Yorktown northeast of Fort Monroe. Nat's mother and sister were temporarily safe somewhere behind there, but Nat believed they would never be truly free until he found them and lead them north into Canada.

When Byrl finished his story, Nat tossed the curry brush into a box nailed to the inside of the barn wall. "Near Yorktown, you say. Thanks, Byrl."

Nat dashed out into the weak April sunlight. He knew his danger upon returning to any Southern, or even Northern, state, but Nat was willing to risk his freedom to try to help his mother and sister to theirs.

Nat ran up to the Quaker's house and knocked on the back door. The bearded farmer had been good to Nat. He could not leave without expressing gratitude for being hired for real money. Nat shivered, and only partly from the crisp Canadian air.

★ ★ ★ ★ ★

Gideon pitched the last forkful of hay into the family cow's manger and sighed with weariness. Helping take care of the barely conscious stranger was hard on Gideon and all his family. William's reminder about the taxes made the situation worse. Gideon glanced longingly at his favorite sanctuary in the haymow. He was tempted to climb up there to write in his journal or maybe read a book. But there were chores to do, even on the Sabbath.

Sighing again, Gideon turned to the two hounds stretched out on old tow sacks by the barn door. "I guess I'd better feed you," he began, but stopped when they leaped up, long ears flopping. They raced out into the late afternoon sunlight and down the long drive, their deep bawling announcing someone's arrival.

"Oh no!" Gideon groaned. Without even looking, he knew Barley Cobb was coming, uninvited, in time for supper. He had periodically done that before Gideon's father died. Since then, Cobb had showed up more often. In Christian charity, the Tugwells invited Cobb to join them even though they barely had enough for themselves.

Gideon didn't like or trust the childless widower, who did some farming but made most of his living with his hounds by catching runaway slaves. Gideon reminded himself to be polite and stepped out of the barn.

He stopped in surprise and stared at the man sliding off the bare back of a brown mule. For the first time that Gideon remembered, Cobb's brown hair was brushed and slicked down with grease. It still hung to his shoulders in back and on the sides, but this was the first time Gideon had ever seen it looking neat. His clothing was also clean, although poorly patched.

Cobb shifted the wad of tobacco from his left cheek and spat, leaving small brown stains on his beard. "Well, howdy, Gideon!" he said heartily, ignoring the hounds sniffing at his polished boots. It was the first time Gideon had seen them without dirt or dust.

The boy was too shocked to reply. He continued to stare as Cobb reached inside his shirt and pulled out some wilted wood ferns. "I was passin' the swamp," Cobb explained, "when I seen these here. Is yore ma to home?"

★ ★

Gideon didn't answer. He was still too surprised at Cobb's appearance.

"Reckon I'll jist go find out fer myself." He grinned, showing brown-stained teeth. "Wish me luck, boy. I could soon be yore new pa, 'cause I'm a-comin' to court yore ma!"

# CHICKEN DINNER
# THREATS

Cobb's surprise announcement distressed and angered Gideon. He was old enough to know that a widow with small children had almost no way to survive except to remarry. He had heard of a desperate case where a destitute woman buried her husband one day and remarried the next.

Gideon did not want his mother to marry anyone, especially the brutal slave catcher. Gideon's older half brother had inherited two-thirds of the Tugwell farm, but Isham would probably turn his share over to his stepmother. However, under state law, if she remarried, her new husband would become the sole property owner.

What angered Gideon most was his conviction that William was behind Cobb's plan to marry his mother. Once married, he would sell the property to William. That would leave the family worse off than they were now.

Gideon didn't get to say anything to his mother or little brother before they all sat down at the table, where Mrs. Tugwell offered the blessing. Before her "amen" was echoed, Gideon opened his eyes and saw Cobb reaching a long arm past the glass now holding the ferns.

Gideon watched in dismay as Cobb ignored the serving fork on the platter of fried chicken and used his fingers to pick up both meaty breast pieces and the gizzard, Gideon's favorites.

"Martha," Cobb said to the hostess, who lifted the platter

★ ★

and passed it to Kate, "after seein' that stranger in there, it's my duty to warn ye about him." Cobb jerked his head toward the boys' closed bedroom door where the sick man slept. "Ye don't know his name nor nothin' about him. It's a mighty big risk fer ye and yore family to let the likes of him stay under yore roof."

"There is no place else for him," Mrs. Tugwell said evenly as Kate took one drumstick and a wing before passing the platter to Lilly. "The doctor said he's going to be all right now that his fever broke, but he's still too weak to be moved, or even talk."

Cobb's hazel eyes under heavy eyebrows locked on Martha Tugwell's blue eyes across the table. "When he's up, will he go peaceable-like, or try to hang around and leech off'a ye, a widder woman?"

Ben leaned closer to Gideon on the bench to whisper, "What's a leech?"

Gideon lowered his voice. "You're lookin' at one."

Their mother scolded, "Boys, whispering isn't polite."

Gideon thought it was more polite than saying aloud what he had just told Ben, but he nodded and watched anxiously as Ben took a wing and the heart.

When Ben passed the platter to Gideon, only a thigh and the bony chicken back remained. It was a temptation to take the thigh, but his mother loved that piece, so Gideon took the bony back and scowled at their "guest."

Cobb chewed with his mouth open. "Martha, far be it from me to mention what folks'll say about ye havin' a strange man—"

"Then don't say it, Mr. Cobb!" she interrupted. "Especially in front of my children!" She took the last piece of chicken without even looking at it.

Cobb licked his fingers, then wiped them on his pants leg before looking at her from under heavy eyebrows. "I'm a plain-spoken man, Martha, so I may as well say in front of these here young'uns what I come to see ye about."

Gideon saw the alarm in his mother's eyes before she protested, "I suspect what you have in mind, Mr. Cobb. I would rather you not speak of it right now."

"Call me Barley," he said, again biting into the piece of chicken. "But it's a man's place to speak and a woman's to keep silent, as the Good Book says."

Gideon knew enough from Sunday school that Cobb was misquoting Paul the apostle. But the boy said nothing, watching the distress in his mother's tired face.

"Mr. Cobb," she began, a hint of impatience in her tone, "I've asked you—"

He broke in. "Barley. Remember? It's more fittin'."

"Mr. Cobb," she replied deliberately, "please talk about something else." She glanced at the children.

"No, Martha, I'll say my piece." There was nothing left except the gnawed chicken breast bone, which Cobb placed on the plate. He reached across the ferns for the mashed potatoes. "Like it says in the Good Book, when a man and woman marries, they become one. But in Virginia, the law says that 'one' is the man."

Gideon glanced at his younger siblings and noticed the puzzled looks on their faces. They didn't understand, but Gideon did. He wanted to defend his mother, but she spoke before he could decide what to do.

"Please, Mr. Cobb! That's enough!"

The slave catcher flinched at her tone, then shook his head. "Ye got no choice, Martha! Yore boy here"—he glanced at Gideon—"cain't handle this farm by hisself. Now, if'n ye was to marry—"

"Mr. Cobb, I'm not going to ask you again! Stop!"

He looked at her as if she had taken leave of her senses. "That's no way to talk to a man who's got a way fer ye to be happy an' go on livin' here."

"Excuse me!" Mrs. Tugwell stood up and threw her napkin

★ ★

on the table. "Mr. Cobb, I've never in my life asked anyone to leave my home, but you've given me no choice. Good night, sir!"

Gideon watched disbelief cross the man's face.

"Good night!" Mrs. Tugwell repeated firmly.

Cobb glanced longingly at his plate, then angrily scowled. "Martha, ye'll be sorry fer this!" When she didn't reply, he rose slowly, his beard twitching where his mouth moved in controlled fury.

Gideon slid off the bench and jerked the back door open. He met Cobb's hard eyes with his own as the man stalked out onto the porch, where the dogs growled at him.

"This ain't over!" Cobb called over his shoulder.

Gideon quickly closed the door, then turned toward his mother. The three smaller children had clustered around her, clinging to her in fright and confusion. Gideon saw tears on her eyelashes and rushed over to throw his arms around her shoulders.

"Oh, children," she whispered, "for all our sakes, I hope I didn't make a mistake!"

★ ★ ★ ★ ★

After another week of vainly trying to obtain the necessary pass, Emily wearily returned to Mrs. Stonum's house and entered the second-story bedchamber she shared with Hannah Chandler. So many people had flocked into Richmond since the war started that housing was almost nonexistent.

"Same old story?" Hannah guessed from where she brushed her hair in front of the dresser mirror. She was a pretty girl of twelve, wearing a high-necked blouse with long sleeves and buttons down the front.

"The same," Emily sadly admitted. She climbed the two short steps on the footstool beside the high canopied bed. Pulling off her worn shoes, she said, "No pass for a Yankee girl. I've worn out my only pair of shoes, and I can't buy new ones because I don't have any money, even if there were any available."

"That's the fault of your Mr. Lincoln," Hannah said sarcastically. "His naval blockade is so tight that our ships can't even dock on our own shores. He's responsible for our terrible inflation, too. Prices are ridiculous."

Emily bit her tongue. She liked Hannah and didn't want to risk another disagreement with her. Hannah blamed Yankees for killing her father at Manassas shortly before her mother died of fever.

Emily said softly, "At least you're earning some money." She dropped both shoes on the wooden floor and rubbed aching arches through her stockings.

"Yes," Hannah agreed. "A whole dollar and a half for twelve hours. Twelve and a half cents an hour isn't much, but not many girls can get jobs of any kind. I'm still sure I can help you get hired there if you want."

Emily hesitated. One cold morning in February she had gone with Hannah to Brown's Island at the foot of Richmond's Seventh Street and the ordnance laboratory, where about seventy women and girls worked.

Those as young as nine were packing filled primers used to touch off charges in Confederate cannons, plus making percussion caps and loading cartridges with gunpowder. It was highly dangerous work. Emily remembered that the only source of heat was a coal-burning stove. She had seen loose powder drifting in the air and feared the stove might set off an explosion.

Hannah's offer was a temptation because Emily had decided she did not like being indebted to Fitzhugh. If she had some money, she could pay him to deliver her letters. But she had a stronger reason to not work with Hannah.

"Thanks," Emily told her, "but I'd be a traitor if I made munitions to be used against my country."

Hannah laid the hairbrush down. She had dark shoulder-length hair parted in the middle so it cascaded down both sides of her face. "You're the only Yankee I would even speak to."

Mrs. Stonum's voice came from the bottom of the stairs. "Emily, I need some assistance in my nursing rounds. Can you help me?"

"Be right there," she called. With a weary sigh, she slid off the high bed onto the steps. She sat on them and reluctantly pulled her shoes back on. "Hannah," she said tiredly, "if I don't get that pass soon, I may have no choice but to take you up on that job possibility."

"Even against your conscience?"

Emily couldn't answer. She hurried downstairs with the question pricking her heart. Now she, like millions of grown-ups, had to make a difficult personal decision. Thousands of men had already died defending their choice; Emily would have to live with hers.

★　★　★　★　★

In the first several days after Nat reentered the Union from Canada, wearing clothing the Quaker had given him, his heart leaped every time a white man looked at him. The fear of being seized and returned to slavery kept him constantly tense. It was worse when some white men looked at him closely, obviously noticing his light honey-colored skin and dark eyes.

The common slouch hat effectively hid his curly black hair, and his unknown white father's facial features helped him pass. His speech and manner did not betray his fugitive status.

He continued south through the Northern states on his quest to find his mother and sister in Virginia. *When I find my mother*, he told himself as he rode through Pennsylvania on a hay wagon driven by a heavyset Dutch farmer, *I'm going to ask her who my white daddy was even though the law says she can't tell anyone.*

"Going far?" the driver asked, clucking to his team of draft horses.

Nat nodded, trying to minimize conversation that might somehow trap him. He couldn't trust anyone because of the Fugitive Slave Law. He was aware that the farmer kept looking at him out of the corner of his eye.

"Seems to me," he said quietly, "I hear the hint of a Southern accent in your voice."

Nat didn't think he had any, but others in Canada had mentioned the same thing. "I guess I picked it up someplace," he replied carefully.

The driver nodded and lightly slapped the reins across the team's backs. "Is it true that in the South some white men have children by slave women and then sell the offspring like chickens or hogs?"

Nat stiffened in alarm. Had the farmer guessed the truth about him? He said noncommittally, "So I've heard."

The farmer didn't say anything else, making Nat even more concerned. He was edgy, ready to leap from the wagon and flee across the neatly tilled fields if necessary.

Nat had secretly resented his unknown father because the law said a child born of a slave woman and a white man was considered black. Nat's father, like countless others in the South, would have claimed the boy if his mother was white. Instead, Nat had been relegated to slave status, a fugitive re-entering the South.

The farmer turned and grinned from under his wide-brimmed hat. "Relax, son. You're safe with me."

Nat wanted to believe him, but he remained alert as the wagon rolled slowly south. There, for sure, every man's hand would be against him. He would have to travel through both Confederate and Union troops. That would require changing identities to be inconspicuous. But there was no turning back, regardless of the dangers ahead.

"Fact is," the farmer said, "if you're a runaway, which I suspect you are, you'd be safe with my friends."

At the word "runaway," Nat had turned to leap from the

★ ★

wagon, but hesitated. He could outrun the heavyset man if need be. "Oh?" Nat tried to sound noncommittal.

"I don't know why you'd go back," the farmer said quietly, "but your chances of making it very far in the South are mighty slim—if you go by land."

Nat said nothing, but waited, still ready to jump and run.

"On the other hand," the farmer said thoughtfully, "if you got on a certain boat I know about, you could get pretty far south in safety. After you dock, of course, I can't say. You interested?"

Nat studied the square face and decided the man looked honest and sincere. "Let's just say I'm curious," Nat said casually. "What do you have in mind?"

"Well, first, I think you've taken leave of your senses, but if you're determined to go, you can soon be cruising down Delaware Bay and on to the Atlantic Ocean."

Nat deliberated in silence. *Is this a trap? Or could he be a conductor for the Underground Railroad? If he is, I'm sure he's never helped a runaway slave go south.*

Nat was as tight as a banjo string before he said, "Tell me about this boat."

★ ★ ★ ★ ★

The sun was high overhead, and Gideon was already so tired that he almost staggered in the crooked furrows his plow made. He didn't have the strength to hold the handles steady enough to make straight grooves as his father had done. Gideon looped the mule's reins over his shoulders so he could grip the plow with both hands. Perspiration dripped off his eyebrows and stung his eyes.

As he often did, he mentally escaped the hated farm chores by thinking of someday when he would be a writer. Meanwhile, he kept a daily journal in which he recorded thoughts, events, descriptions, and scraps of story ideas. But no matter how hard he tried, the words never seemed quite right. He had often said

★ ★

wistfully to his mother, *"If there was just one person who could tell me what I'm doing wrong . . ."*

His musings were suddenly jarred by the clanging of a bell from the distant Tugwell house.

"Whoa, Hercules!" Gideon called out and turned to listen, half in hope, half in concern. A bell salvaged from an abandoned church rang out clearly in the air. Once. Twice. Three times. Pause. Repeat.

"Time to eat," Gideon told the mule. He unhitched the animal and rode him bareback to the barn. Gideon was too weary to walk, but he didn't want his mother to know. He glanced at the old bell mounted on a post. His mother or sisters rang it when the noonday meal was nearly ready. In emergencies, it had been rung to summon Gideon's father from the fields.

Ben was at the outside bench washing up with homemade lye soap and water in an old gray basin as Gideon approached. Ben asked, "You ever make chicken roosts when Papa was alive?"

"Many times," Gideon replied, pulling up his sleeves and throwing his brother's dirty water in a wide sweep across the yard. Unfenced chickens squawked in surprise and ran away with half-flapping wings.

"Well," Ben muttered through the old sacking he was using as a towel, "I'm too worn-out to—"

He broke off when Kate burst through the back door and yelled, "Come quick! Mama wants you!"

Gideon dropped the pan and dashed toward the door, which Kate held open. It took a moment for his eyes to adjust to the change from brilliant sunlight to the soft interior of the house. Then he made out his mother and both sisters at the door to the boys' room. The one-handed man sagged weakly against the doorframe.

"Sir, you shouldn't be up!" Mrs. Tugwell exclaimed.

"I'm . . ." he began, but stopped as his legs slowly buckled under him.

★ ★

"Boys," she cried, "help me get him back to bed!"

Gideon and Ben and their mother assisted the stranger back to the lower bunk bed. Gideon told himself, *Now we'll find out who he is and why he's here.*

★ ★

# BLUNDERS OF
# THE LIPS

The boys' small bedroom was packed. Ben and the two sisters perched on the top bunk, while Gideon and his mother sat on the bottom one. All eagerly waited for the stranger to speak from the opposite bunk, where Isham had slept before he went off to war.

The stranger was thin and wiry, just under six feet tall, with disheveled dark brown hair falling over light blue eyes. "Where . . . where am I?" he asked weakly.

"At our farm," Mrs. Tugwell replied. "We're the Tugwells. I'm Martha. These are my children—Gideon, Ben, Kate, and Lilly."

The stranger nodded briefly to each in turn before Mrs. Tugwell added, "Forgive me, but when you first came, I had Gideon look for some identification on you, but he didn't find any."

"My name's Fletcher—John Fletcher." His voice was low and weak, as though speaking was difficult.

Gideon said, "From your uniform, we figured you must have been with our troops."

"Was." Fletcher raised his handless left arm before glancing around the tiny room. "How . . . how long have I been here?"

"Ten days," Mrs. Tugwell told him.

"Ten. . . ?" He seemed startled. "I'm sorry to have inconvenienced you."

★ ★

She said, "You had a terrible fever. Sometimes you muttered, but we didn't understand the words."

"I guess I was out of my head."

Kate piped up. "Where you from?"

"The Shenandoah."

"If you'll give us the name and address of your family, we'll notify them—" Mrs. Tugwell stopped herself at the sudden puckering of his face.

"They're all dead," Fletcher said dully, turning his face away. "My wife, my little boy. Everyone." His voice broke and his thin body shook with silent sobs.

"I'm terribly sorry, Mr. Fletcher," Gideon's mother said softly. She motioned for the children to leave.

Fletcher turned toward her and said hoarsely, "You stay, please. You have a right to know."

The four Tugwell siblings stepped outside and closed the door. They were silent, deeply touched by the plight of the stranger. Gideon walked out onto the back porch, trailed by his brother and sisters. They sat on the top step, silently waiting for their mother to come out with John Fletcher's story, and why he was here.

★　★　★　★　★

Nat listened carefully to the Pennsylvania farmer tell about how a boat would take him back to Virginia. The runaway slave had never been on a boat, yet he could see his chances of being caught were less there than if he tried to cross overland. But could he trust the farmer? Was he a conductor for the Underground Railroad? Or was he sending Nat into a trap?

Nat thought about his mother and sister somewhere in a Yankee military camp on Virginia's peninsula. If he could locate them, he could probably help them be sent north to freedom as he had been. If he was caught, he would again be a slave, and chances were strong that he would never again see either of them.

★　★

But if he succeeded, he would be encouraged to continue his quest for his three younger brothers. It seemed like an impossible goal, but Nat wanted more than anything in the world to reunite his family.

He turned to the farmer on the seat beside him. "I've decided. How do I get on that boat?"

★ ★ ★ ★ ★

Gideon, Ben, Kate, and Lilly were still impatiently waiting for news about John Fletcher when the two hounds exploded from under the high porch and began barking.

"Somebody's coming," Lilly said, leaping up and following the dogs as they raced around the corner of the house and down the long dirt driveway.

"It'd better not be Barley Cobb," Ben muttered.

"I don't think he'd dare come around," Gideon said, standing and starting after his little sister. "It's more likely to be William Lodge."

Ben, Kate, and Gideon ran along the side of the drive, trailing behind the hounds and Lilly. Gideon called to the dogs, "Rock! Red! Quiet!" They broke off their baying, and the boy shaded his eyes against the sun.

At first, he didn't recognize the slender man in his mid-thirties driving a two-wheeled gig. The new arrival reined in the dapple gray horse when the four children reached him.

"Good day, Tugwells," he said cheerfully. "Remember me? Oliver Fitzhugh. I used to be a Temperance speaker around here before the war."

Gideon remembered seeing the man in the village. "How are you, Mr. Fitzhugh?" Gideon replied.

"Fine! Just fine! I'm sorry to hear about your father."

Gideon nodded but didn't want to talk about it because there was still too much pain.

"I'm delivering mail to help out our struggling Confederate postal system," Fitzhugh continued. He reached into a wooden box on the floor beside his feet. "Got two letters for you, Gideon."

Mail at the Tugwell home was so rare that all of the children except Gideon squealed excitedly. Gideon merely waited, his pulse quickening because he knew the letters had to be from Emily.

Ben and both sisters crowded around as he took the letters and quickly shoved them inside his shirt. All three siblings protested together, asking whom the letters were from. Gideon ignored his family and quietly thanked Fitzhugh.

"You're welcome," he replied, then asked, "You got any letters you want me to deliver?"

Gideon wouldn't admit that he didn't have money to mail the letters he had written to Emily. "Not today."

Fitzhugh nodded. "Any news around your house?"

There was, but Gideon wouldn't tell about his mother's desperate financial situation or what William warned would happen if the taxes weren't paid when due. Neither would Gideon say anything about Cobb trying to marry his mother. He was even hesitant to mention the stranger, for these were all personal family matters.

"I can't say that there is any," Gideon replied carefully, eager to read Emily's letters in private.

Fitzhugh asked, "Has Isham been in any more battles with the treacherous Yankees?"

"Haven't heard from him," Gideon replied.

"Too bad." Fitzhugh shook his head. "My next stop is at Briarstone Plantation. I thought maybe you'd have something of interest I might tell them."

Gideon shrugged but didn't speak. He certainly wasn't going to pass along anything to William Lodge.

"Just thought I'd ask." Fitzhugh took the reins in hand and prepared to slap them along the horse's back.

Little Lilly piped up. "We got a man in our house."

★ ★

"Oh?" Fitzhugh dropped the reins and fixed intent gray eyes on the little girl.

"He was a wounded soldier who came down sick with a fever," Gideon said hastily. "He's better now. Well, thanks again for the letters." He turned to his siblings and motioned for them to return to the house.

Gideon didn't look back, but he sensed that Fitzhugh was reluctant to leave without more information. Gideon sighed with relief when he heard the gig's wheels start to move and the hounds again began baying.

"Lilly," Gideon whispered fiercely to her, "I wish you could learn not to blurt things out!"

"Why?" she demanded innocently. "What did I do?"

He took her hand and gave it a gentle squeeze. "Never mind." He added to all his siblings, "I'm going to the barn. You stay here. Call me when Mama comes out."

"You're going there to read those letters, and I know why!" Kate said smugly. "They're from Emily Lodge!"

"Doesn't matter who they're from," Gideon said. He forgot about Fitzhugh and even the one-handed stranger and hurried toward the barn.

Kate started chanting, "Gideon's got a girlfriend! Gideon's got—"

"Children!" their mother's voice interrupted Kate. Standing in the half-open back door, Mrs. Tugwell said, "Please come in and hear why Mr. Fletcher came here."

Sighing, Gideon patted the letters inside his shirt. As much as he longed to read them, they would have to wait. He followed his brother and sisters to the house.

"Shh!" their mother whispered as they entered. "He's still very weak, but he's going to be all right."

Kate asked, "What did he say?"

Mrs. Tugwell motioned for the children to quietly slide onto the wooden benches on both sides of the table. She took her usual place closest to the stove before answering. "He was in

★ ★

the same regiment as Isham, so when Mr. Fletcher received a medical discharge, Isham sent a message for us."

"How is Isham?" Gideon asked. He felt as close to his older half brother as he did to his other siblings.

"He's fine. He's fully recovered from his wound suffered at Manassas and just wanted us to know that."

"That's great!" Gideon exclaimed in relief. "But what about him?" Gideon motioned with his head toward the closed bedroom door.

Mrs. Tugwell straightened a lock of hair that had fallen across her eyes. "Invading Yankees burned his place and killed his brother."

"Oh, how awful!" Kate exclaimed.

"Yes," her mother agreed. "You heard him say his wife and son were dead. His mother died a few years ago, and his father suffocated last year when a load of hay overturned on him. Mr. Fletcher was already in the militia, so with nothing left, he joined the army. That's where he met Isham."

Gideon shook his head. Death was so common, but nobody ever got used to the pain of losing someone close.

"What about his hand?" Ben wanted to know.

"Lost it after the Battle of Manassas. It took a long time to heal; then he was discharged. He planned to come by and tell us about Isham, then go on back to the Shenandoah. But there was fever in the camp—"

"And he caught it." Gideon interrupted. "There's always fever in the camps! When I last saw Isham, he said more soldiers die from disease than Yankee guns!"

Mrs. Tugwell said soberly, "Mr. Fletcher wants to move on as soon as he's well, but . . ." She hesitated, seemingly uncomfortable in continuing.

"But what?" Gideon prompted.

"He has nothing left in this world, and you boys need help," his mother explained. "You're both so overworked that I'm afraid you're going to get sick. Then we would certainly lose

★ ★

this place, and William will get it."

"Never!" Gideon cried. "You know how I hate farming, but Papa would never want William to get our home! I won't let Papa and you down. Ben and I will make it work!"

A sudden brightness showed in his mother's eyes. She reached across the table and gripped his hand. "Thank you," she whispered hoarsely. "I know you mean it, but we really need a man's help, so maybe—"

"No!" Gideon burst out. "Nobody can take Papa's place—especially not Barley Cobb!"

His mother blinked in surprise. "I think you're misunderstanding me," she said softly. "Now, here's what I have in mind. . . ."

★ ★ ★ ★ ★

Emily finished drying the last dish in Mrs. Stonum's spacious kitchen with good fragrances of dinner still lingering in the air. There was something about the room that reminded Emily of her mother. She, too, had been a good cook. A warm, caring woman, she had been crushed with grief two years ago when scarlet fever claimed the lives of both her sons within one week.

Emily hadn't meant to become melancholy, but her heart suddenly ached from remembering how disease claimed the lives of her father, mother, and two younger brothers. Even though her only living relatives were at Briarstone, Emily longed to return to Illinois, where her best friend lived. It was the closest thing Emily had to "home," and Jessie Barlow was like a sister.

She wasn't aware that she had bent over the dishpan, silently weeping, until she heard Hannah's voice behind her.

"You all right, Emily?"

Embarrassed, she wiped the tears with the hem of her apron and nodded without turning around.

"You got turned down again for a pass?" Hannah asked,

★ ★

coming around to see Emily's face.

"Yes, but that wasn't what upset me."

"What, then? Thinking about your family?"

Emily nodded. "Yes. I try to keep it from hurting so much, but sometimes . . ." her voice broke.

"I know," Hannah said gently. "I hate being an orphan, too. But at least you and I are old enough that we don't have to be put in one of those homes."

Emily sighed heavily and began putting the dishes into the cupboard. "I guess we should be grateful for that." She motioned toward the back of the stove. "I kept your food warm."

"Thanks." Hannah lifted a plate and flatware from those Emily had washed and approached the stove. "One of the girls quit today, so there's an opening at work."

"I appreciate it. I sure need that twelve and a half cents an hour very much, and I thought a lot about it after the last time you mentioned it. But I also thought of Brice, my girl friend's brother, and decided I just can't make anything that might kill him or any other of my people."

Hannah shrugged. "Suit yourself." She lifted the lid on the pot at the back of the stove. "You've mentioned this Brice several times. How old is he?"

"He must be nineteen by now."

"You like him?"

The question caught Emily by surprise. "Back home, he was always teasing Jessie and me."

Hannah slid a chunk of bacon onto her plate and added a slice of cornbread. "That doesn't answer my question. You like him?"

"I'm not old enough to be interested in boys."

"Lots of girls marry when they're fourteen or fifteen. You're certainly old enough to be interested."

Emily squirmed a little. She remembered how Brice had written her, asking her to pray for him. And how handsome he looked when she had seen him once near Briarstone, wearing

★ ★

his cavalry uniform. She felt her cheeks warm at the memory of what he had said that day.

Hannah started to sit down at the table with her food, then stared at Emily. "Are you blushing?"

"No, of course not!" Emily turned her back and resumed putting dishes into the cupboard.

"You are, too!" Hannah cried with delight. "What made you do that?"

Emily liked Hannah, so she decided to share what Brice had told his friends in her presence. "I ran into him once by accident near my cousins' place. Brice said that he was going to marry me when I grow up."

"No!" Hannah grinned broadly. "He didn't!"

Emily nodded, feeling her face flush even more. "He was just teasing, sort of like a big brother. He used to do that back home when I visited his sister."

Hannah asked, "Have you heard from him lately?"

"No. But you know how the mail is these days."

"What about this Gideon Tugwell you've told me about? How do you feel about him?"

"We're friends. I like to talk to him. I wrote him a couple of letters, but he hasn't answered—" She stopped herself, but it was too late.

"How'd you get money to do that?"

Emily realized she had trapped herself. She could not tell anyone about her arrangement with Oliver Fitzhugh—not even Hannah. Emily desperately tried to think of how to answer that without telling a lie. "I . . . I can't say," she finally admitted.

Hannah's eyes narrowed. "I thought we were friends."

"We are!"

"But not enough to share *some* secrets, huh?"

The sudden coolness in Hannah's tone hurt Emily. "It's not that," she protested. "It's just that . . . I can't, that's all."

★ ★

"I see." Hannah turned back to her food and wordlessly began eating.

Emily groaned softly, hung up the dish towel, and hurried from the room. *Now I've done it. She's suspicious, and maybe I've even lost her as a friend.*

★ ★

# THOUGHTS
# ABOUT SLAVERY

Gideon's family waited until John Fletcher gained more strength before Mrs. Tugwell put their idea before him. After supper, he took her suggestion and eased into the old chair by the fireplace, where her husband used to sit. She sat in her hickory rocker facing him. The children seated themselves on the hardwood floor and leaned against the wall.

Fletcher listened quietly as Mrs. Tugwell outlined the plan she had discussed with her children. "So," she concluded, "you say you feel well enough to move on even though you're still weak. But move on to what? You said there is nobody or nothing left in the Shenandoah for you."

"That's true, but—"

"Please hear me out. Gideon and Ben are doing a man's work, but it's not enough. They need an experienced farmer like you to help. We have no money to pay you, but a place in the barn can be fixed up for you to live in, and we'll feed you. What do you say?"

Gideon leaned forward, aware of his tired and aching muscles, watching Fletcher's eyes.

He replied, "I'm obliged to all of you, but—" he lifted his left arm where it ended in a scarred wrist.

"But nothing!" Mrs. Tugwell interrupted. "No matter where you go or what you do, you'll learn to live with that wound. You will be no less a man because of it."

★ ★

Gideon sensed that his mother was trying not to sound desperate, but he knew how very much help was needed if they were going to be able to keep the farm.

Fletcher asked softly, "You really believe that?"

"Yes, I do," Gideon's mother answered.

Slowly, Fletcher let his eyes move searchingly from her to each of the children. His gaze settled on Gideon. "You support your mother in this?"

Gideon didn't want anyone to try taking his father's place, but the lines on his mother's face had deepened lately. Like other widows Gideon had seen, she was being rushed into old age before her time. "Yes," Gideon said, thinking of Barley Cobb as the alternative, "we all do."

Fletcher didn't speak for several seconds. When he did, his eyes were bright. "I am touched," he said softly, "and I can never repay all of you for the way you took care of me while I was helpless. So I'll stay around until I've somewhat repaid you for your kindness. But after the crops are gathered in this fall, I'll move on."

Glancing at his mother, Gideon thought the lines in her tired face had suddenly deepened in disappointment. "Move on, Mr. Fletcher?" she asked quietly.

"I think it's best," he replied, "for many reasons."

For a moment there was silence. Then the two hounds suddenly barked and rushed from under the back porch. They bayed loudly as they raced down the lane.

"My stars!" Mrs. Tugwell exclaimed. "Who could that be this time of evening?"

Ben grinned. "If it's Barley Cobb, he's missed supper this time and he'll be plenty mad."

Gideon didn't think it likely that the slave catcher would come around again after Mrs. Tugwell had ordered him off the place. Still, curiosity made Gideon get to his feet. He headed outside, trailed by his siblings.

Darkness prevented seeing anything more than coal-oil

lamps on an approaching carriage. "Well, it's not Cobb," Gideon told his brother. "He only rides a mule." Gideon wondered what Cobb would do when he found out that Fletcher was going to stay on at the Tugwell farm.

The team stopped in response to a soft feminine voice saying, "Whoa!"

"A woman!" Gideon exclaimed. He raised his voice to the hounds. "Rock! Red! Come here! Come on!"

The weak light of the carriage lamps cast the dogs' shadows as they obeyed. The driver stood up so that the lights briefly touched her face.

"It's Mrs. Yates!" Gideon cried, hurrying toward her with his brother and sisters trailing.

Clara Yates and her husband owned the local newspaper, the *Church Creek Villager*. They also did some farming with the aid of former slaves, whom they had freed, and it was whispered around that they were abolitionists.

Gideon could not guess why Mrs. Yates had come to visit them. She had never done so before.

"Good evening, children," the visitor said as Ben took the reins from her and tied them to the hitching post. "Is your mother home?"

They assured her in a happy chorus that she was and escorted her into the small wooden house. The lamplight showed she was matronly, about sixty, barely five feet tall, with beautiful silver hair parted in the middle.

Mrs. Tugwell introduced her to Fletcher, briefly told why he was there, then invited Mrs. Yates to sit in the hickory rocker.

Gideon's mother said, "I'm sorry not to be able to offer you coffee or tea. The Union blockade, you know, has almost stopped imports of such things."

"It's quite all right, Martha," their guest said, her deep blue eyes lingering on Fletcher from behind wire-rimmed glasses.

★ ★

"I can only stay a moment." Her gaze shifted to Gideon, but she spoke to his mother.

"Martha, I've read the pieces you gave me that Gideon wrote. . . ."

"What?" he exclaimed in surprise. He turned anguished eyes to his mother. "Mama! You didn't!"

"I was proud of your writing, but I wanted someone who really knew about such things to judge them."

"Ah, Mama!" Gideon groaned, so embarrassed that he closed his eyes and dropped his head. "I wrote those only for myself . . . and you!"

"I'm sorry," she cried, coming to him and trying to put her arms around him. "I didn't think you'd mind."

Gideon drew back from her even though he knew the action hurt her feelings. He just couldn't help himself.

"Excuse me," Mrs. Yates said quickly. "Gideon, I know how sensitive a boy your age can be, but your mother was right to show those pages to me. You have potential, and I'd like to encourage you."

Gideon stared in disbelief. "I do?"

"You certainly do. Oh, you have some problems with grammar and punctuation, but you have a feel and the heart for good writing. The rest can be learned."

He knew his mouth had dropped open, but he couldn't get anything to come out of it. *I have potential!*

Mrs. Yates smiled knowingly and turned to Fletcher. "While our young aspiring author composes himself, let me ask you a few questions, Mr. Fletcher. I suspect there's a story in you that readers would like to know about. . . ."

Gideon didn't really hear much more. He grabbed Ben around the neck and gave him a brotherly hug. "You hear that?" Gideon whispered. "I'm not just dreaming! Someday I will be a writer in spite of everything."

Ben didn't reply, but Mrs. Yates did. "Dreams are only the beginning in life, Gideon. With your mother's permission, I'll

★ ★

show you some of the necessary steps to achieving your dreams. I'd like you to write a column for the paper, for which I'll pay a modest amount."

"Pay?" Gideon's voice shot up. "Pay me for. . . ?" His voice broke and he couldn't continue.

"Not much," Mrs. Yates replied. "Call it stamp money, for someday, if you develop the way I believe you will, I'll give you the names of some editors in Richmond to whom you can mail your work."

Gideon swallowed hard. Send his writing to a big Richmond newspaper! The idea added still more joy to Gideon's sudden good fortune. He could also write Emily!

Almost giddy with all this unexpected opportunity, Gideon exclaimed, "Thanks very much, Mrs. Yates!"

Overcome with excitement, he slipped out onto the back porch and looked up to the sky. "Thanks!" he whispered. "Thanks from the bottom of my heart!"

Suddenly, doubt seized Gideon. *What if I fail? What if I can't really do it?* Misgivings drove all happiness from him. He stood in the hot night feeling only cold fear.

★　★　★　★　★

The tension in the bedroom Emily shared with Hannah grew all week until Emily decided to do something about it. As the girls prepared for bed in strained silence, Emily put down her hairbrush and turned from the mirror.

"I don't like this tension between us. Can we please talk about it?"

"There's nothing to talk about." Hannah settled her threadbare nightgown over her head. "Friends don't keep secrets from each other."

"It's not my choice," Emily protested, trying to control her distress. "I've tried to tell you that I can't talk about it. It's out of my hands."

"You could tell me. I can keep a secret."

★　★

"That's not the point. I can't betray a confidence."

Hannah climbed the two short steps to sit on the edge of her high canopied bed. "Does this have anything to do with you trying to get a pass through our lines?"

"No, it's nothing like that."

Hannah persisted. "Does it have anything to do with President Davis declaring martial law in Richmond and arresting pro-Northern sympathizers on charges of saying or doing something against the Confederacy?"

"Not that, either."

Hannah slid under the top sheet and angrily pounded the pillow. "But you're a Yankee, and you haven't kept it a secret that you're for Lincoln. Since President Davis suspended what they call *habeas* . . . something . . ."

"*Corpus,*" Emily said, "*habeas corpus.*"

Hannah nodded. "Yes, that. Anyway, some men have been put in jail for something they said. The way I understand it, under this *habeas* rule, those men don't even have to be brought before a judge."

"That's right. They can be held without trial."

"So," Hannah said, "could you get locked up because of whatever your secret is?"

Emily was annoyed at the stubborn way Hannah kept probing. "I've never heard of a thirteen-year-old girl being arrested under martial law or that *habeas corpus.*"

"Me, either, but that doesn't mean it couldn't happen. If I come home from work one night and you're not here, I'll bet they've locked you up."

"That's a terrible thing to say!" Emily exclaimed, giving her long golden hair vigorous strokes with the brush. It was bad enough that the Confederate authorities kept refusing her request for a pass so she could return to Illinois. That frustrated her. So did the lack of money in a city where wartime shortages and the Union coastal blockade had sent inflation shooting up.

"Maybe it is," Hannah admitted, "but I'm your only friend

★ ★

in this city besides Mrs. Stonum. Does she know?"

When Emily shook her head, Hannah continued. "If you're keeping secrets from both of us, what are you keeping from the provost marshal?"

*Nothing!* The angry word sprang to Emily's lips, but she bit it back. She forced herself to say calmly, "I'll eventually get my pass, and I won't betray a confidence. Now, please! Let it go and let's be friends."

"Not until you tell me how you're getting letters delivered without having any money."

Emily took a deep breath, put down the hairbrush, and approached the nightstand by her bed. She bent over the glass chimney, feeling the warmth of the small flame in the kerosene lamp for a second before she blew out the light. "I've already said all I'm going to about that."

"Well," Hannah's voice came through the darkness that settled over the room, "I'm not through."

Emily didn't answer but turned her eyes toward the ceiling and breathed an anguished sigh.

★　★　★　★　★

Late at night, days after being smuggled aboard a merchant steamer by the Pennsylvania farmer, Nat heard the side paddle wheels slow to a stop. At first, he feared that maybe one of the Union gunboats had caught the blockade runner he was hiding on. Then he relaxed as he recognized the captain's measured step outside the small cabin.

The door opened, and the burly officer's bearded face showed in the whale-oil lamplight. "We're here. Follow me quietly."

Wordlessly, Nat trailed the big man onto the deck, which was in total darkness. Guiding himself by running his hand along the rail, Nat stayed a step behind the captain until he stopped.

★　★

He whispered, "You'll have to jump. Can you see the wharf?"

Nat stared into the night, barely discerning the outline of a wooden dock strewn with hogsheads and bales of cotton and tobacco. "Yes," he answered softly. "But first, where are we?"

"In Mobjack Bay. I can't risk running closer to Yorktown. You'll have to cross west to the York River toward Williamsburg or follow the York's western shore to Yorktown. By now, Yankees may have taken both places."

The captain's huge rough hand briefly clasped the teen's right one. "Watch out for patrollers. I hope you find your mother and sister."

"Thanks." Nat cautiously stepped to the space where there was no railing. He crouched, then leaped into the night toward the Virginia landing.

★　★　★　★　★

As he did every day, Gideon awoke automatically at the first hint of coming daylight. He loved the dawn, when only he and the stars were out, and especially Sunday, when the family observed the Sabbath. His sore muscles could rest for a few hours.

He quietly dressed in the darkened room to avoid waking his brother or John Fletcher. With Emily's letters again inside his homespun shirt, and carrying his heavy work brogans, Gideon tiptoed on stockinged feet from the bedroom. Somehow he would save part of the money Mrs. Yates would pay for his writing so he could soon answer Emily's letters.

He could hear his mother stirring behind her closed bedroom door, but there was no sound from the girls in the lean-to. The stars were fading as Gideon sat on the top step of the back porch and pulled on his shoes. He lit the lantern, lifted the milk pail from the shelf, and headed for the barn, the two hounds trailing him.

The rooster's first crow sounded as Gideon slid the barn door open enough to squeeze through. He was greeted by the fragrance of hay and the warm smells of the family cow and the big mule. After hanging the bucket and lantern on separate wall pegs, Gideon quickly forked some hay into the manger for the animals before again reading Emily's letters. They were starting to come apart where they had been unfolded and folded so often.

The lantern didn't give much light, but it was enough. Gideon had almost memorized Emily's words. She was well but not having any success in obtaining the necessary pass through Confederate lines to the North. Still, her faith remained high, and she would keep trying to get home to see her best friend, Jessie.

One part of the second letter bothered Gideon. He read it again, frowning. *Remember soon after we met, you told me that slavery seemed natural, but you had never thought much about it one way or another?*

Gideon remembered. It was shortly after the war started and before Yankees had invaded Virginia. Gideon had taken his ax down to the river bottom when Rock and Red bayed at Emily and her cousin Julie, who had wandered onto Tugwell land. Emily had urged him to think about it. His eyes returned to her letter.

*I go with Mrs. Stonum to help on the nursing calls she makes on Richmond people because the doctors are all working with the soldiers. She and some of the grown-ups say it is now clear that the war is no longer really about President Lincoln keeping the Union together, or states' rights, as the Confederates claim. They say it's changing to really be about slavery. What do you think?*

"What *do* I think?" Gideon muttered to himself while carefully refolding the page and sliding it back inside his shirt. *She'll expect me to answer.* He lifted the short three-legged milking stool and the bucket and approached the cow's right side. He sat down on the stool and began milking.

*Black people. Slaves. I don't want to write about that. I*

★ ★

*want to tell Emily the news about my writing.*

The double streams of milk hit the bottom of the empty pail and splattered. Gideon didn't notice. He milked automatically, subconsciously hearing the sound in the pail change as the liquid climbed higher and foam formed. Emily's question troubled him. What *did* he think?

★ ★

# YANKEES
# THREATEN
# RICHMOND

On Nat's first morning back on Virginia soil, he was alert to the danger of being caught as a runaway slave. If captured, he would be returned to Briarstone Plantation to be punished by William. If that was to happen, the beating would surely be worse than the one he got right before he ran away.

It was a temptation to hide during the day and travel at night, but that was not the best way to try finding his mother and sister. He had no clear idea of where they were, except that it was somewhere in a Union camp near Yorktown on Virginia's peninsula.

He was still wearing his cast-off white man's clothes and hat when he arrived there. After sleeping a few hours in a grove of trees, he boldly started walking in full daylight. He was soon startled to see many fine carriages filled with white women, children, and a few old men, all heading north.

Nat had never seen white refugees, but he guessed they were fleeing Yankee invasion troops headed up the peninsula toward Richmond.

That meant the Federal lines were south of where he stood. He turned that way and continued walking, staying well away from the irregular caravan of fugitive whites.

At a bend in the dusty road, he saw a column of slaves trudging ahead of an overloaded wagon of women and children. Nat looked past the two old worn-out mules that pulled the wagon. Those inside had thrown back the canvas top. Nat could see at least a dozen children and a few old women. They were also headed north without a white master or mistress in sight.

Quickly removing his hat so his curly black hair showed, Nat approached the three people walking in front of the others. All eyes focused on Nat, but no one spoke. A boy of about twelve had a bulging pillowcase suspended on a stick over his shoulder. The sturdy-looking man and the matronly woman each carried a large bundle. Nat was sure these were bed sheets that had been confiscated to hold personal belongings.

The adults glanced suspiciously from Nat's white man's clothes to his hair, then looked away. The boy met Nat's eyes, so he asked, "How far to Yorktown?"

The boy shrugged. "Long walk dat way." He pointed south.

Nat nodded. He knew that Yorktown was sixty miles from Richmond at the mouth of the York River. "How close are the Yankees?"

"Too close. Dey ketch ye, dey say ye free, den dey make ye wo'k like ol' massa done. 'Cou'se, dey pay so ye ain't no slave, but it feel de same. Y'all best run."

After entering Union lines, Nat would be safe from William, but apparently the Yankees were forcing fugitive slaves to work, probably in building fortifications.

If that happened, he would not be able to continue his search for his mother and sister. Even if he remained free, how would it be possible to find his family among so many camps? Deciding he had no choice, he ignored the dire warnings shouted after him and again turned south.

★ ★ ★ ★ ★

Gideon's elation over being asked to write a column for the local newspaper soon turned to dismay. He rose early as usual and slipped out onto the back porch. He lit the lantern while both hounds padded up the steps and flopped heavily at his feet.

★ ★

He sat on an upturned wooden hogshead and poised his pencil over the paper, but nothing came. Not a word. He thought of countless topics, but nothing he wanted to write about. Instead, his mind jumped about like a summer grasshopper pursued by the old red rooster.

*Emily. I've got to answer her letter about slavery. The stranger—John Fletcher. He's getting better, so maybe he can soon help Ben and me with the chores. I can't let William Lodge get this place, no matter how much I hate farming. As for Barley Cobb . . .*

"Are you all right, Gideon?" His mother's voice came softly from the open back door where she was outlined by the kerosene lamp on the kitchen table.

"Fine," he replied, "except I can't think of anything to write about for the paper."

She came to him and gently rested her hand on his thin shoulder. "It's the Sabbath, so you rest. You'll think of something tomorrow. Just let your imagination go, like you did when you wrote about the star caught in a mud puddle. That was beautiful."

"Thanks, Mama, but I'm fresh out of ideas."

"I wish I could help, but I don't know how, except to say I know you can do it."

They fell silent while the eastern sky slowly grew brighter. Gideon could barely discern the outbuildings: the chicken house, pigpen, barn, harness shed, scattered farm equipment, and even the well and cistern. He didn't feel like writing about them.

His mother mused, "Yesterday I noticed that the roses are budding."

Gideon hadn't observed them, although he was aware that the lilies of the valley, lilacs, and crocuses were already in bloom. He suddenly remembered that it had been about this same time last year that his father had talked of letting his then eighteen-year-old son, Isham, enlist to fight the Yankees.

★ ★

Gideon felt his mother's fingers tighten on his shoulder. He glanced up as she turned her face away, but not before he saw tears reflected in the lantern light.

Standing quickly, he slipped his arms around her shoulders and laid his head against her cheek. "You're thinking of Papa, aren't you?"

She nodded and whispered, "I miss him so!"

Gideon had to swallow before he could reply, "Me too." He continued to hold her while her shoulders shook with grief. He didn't know what to say, so he just tried to comfort her by holding her tighter.

Slowly, he felt her tremors slacken. She freed herself from his arms and dabbed at her eyes with the corner of her apron. Turning to face him, she said softly, "No one can ever take his place . . . ever. But—"

Gideon tensed, sensing what she was about to say but not wanting to hear it. "I know, Mama. Nobody can take his place for me, either."

That was true, even though he had seldom heard his father praise him for anything. His usual method was to complain and find fault, but Gideon couldn't blame him. Gideon's hatred of the farm had made him seek escape in dreaming of stories, of mentally writing the thoughts that formed in his head. *"Chasing butterflies,"* his father had called it when Gideon dreamed and let the farm work lag.

His mother broke into his thoughts. "Gideon, you're old enough to know that I have no way to support you children except to remarry."

"No!" The word exploded from his mouth so loudly that the hounds raised their heads with startled low whoofs and flapping of long ears. "No, Mama!"

"Please don't make it any more difficult than it already is," she pleaded, taking his hand. "I have prayed about this so often, seeking another way. But there is none. For you children, I must do what has to be done. I have no choice."

★ ★

Gideon's heart cried out in protest, but she was right. He was old enough to understand. He licked dry lips before asking, "But . . . who?"

"I've thought of every eligible man I know at church and in the village, and there's not a single one." She paused, looking at Gideon with eyes pleading to be understood. "No one except—"

"No! Not Barley Cobb! No, Mama! No!"

The hounds leaped up and growled uncertainly at the sudden distress in Gideon's voice.

Fifty yards away, the barn door slid open, causing Gideon and his mother to glance that way. John Fletcher held a lantern high and called, "Is something wrong?"

When he had recovered enough to help, he and Gideon had built two walls in a corner of the barn to close in a twelve-foot-square area for Fletcher's living quarters. Gideon had been fascinated by the way Fletcher had pressed his stump of a wrist against a board to help keep it in place while Gideon held the peg. Fletcher had used his right hand to hammer the peg.

Mrs. Tugwell raised her voice. "No, Mr. Fletcher, nothing's wrong. I'm sorry we disturbed you."

"You didn't," he assured her. "I was awake and feeding the stock when I heard Gideon and the dogs."

"Then come take breakfast with us," she said.

"Thank you. I'll finish forking some hay into the manger, then I'll be in." Fletcher reentered the barn.

Gideon's mother turned to him. "We'll finish our conversation later, but in the meantime, you mustn't say a word to anyone about this. Do you understand?"

"Yes, Mama."

"Good! Now, you'd better put your pencil away. It'll be time to leave for church before long."

Gideon silently watched her enter the house while he stood still, his insides fiercely churning over what she had said about having to remarry. He violently shook his head, crumpled the

★ ★

blank sheet of paper, and threw it and the pencil into the flower bed.

★　★　★　★　★

With Mrs. Stonum between them, Emily and Hannah walked in strained silence along Franklin Street toward Fifth Street's Second Presbyterian Church, where General "Stonewall" Jackson worshiped when he wasn't playing cat and mouse with the Yankees in the Shenandoah Valley. Emily had not been able to lessen Hannah's severe antagonism toward her. She didn't want to attend church with anyone holding hard feelings about her, yet she was unable to think what else she could say or do to end the tension with Hannah.

Mrs. Stonum inadvertently opened the way for Emily to try again. Glancing over the capital, Mrs. Stonum sighed and said, "It's hard to believe this beautiful old city may soon be bombarded or even fall to the invaders."

Hannah scoffed, "Ah, President Davis won't let Yankees get this far!"

"I hope you're right," the widow replied, "but the signs are not good. They're closing in by land and water. After that Union general McClellan transferred his Army of the Potomac from Alexandria to Fort Monroe, he overran Yorktown sixty miles from here. Then he took Williamsburg before our men were able to evacuate Norfolk with its naval yards. That left our ironclad, the *Virginia*, which the Yankees call *Merrimack*, with no base. So she had to be scuttled by her own crew. Now the Federal navy with its ironclad, *Monitor*, is steaming up the James River toward Drewry's Bluff barely eight miles away, and it seems nothing can stop them."

Emily had heard all this, but hearing it summarized so briefly gave her a new appreciation for the danger now fast approaching Richmond.

"General Joe Johnston will stop them," Hannah said bravely. "Everyone at work says so."

★　★

Mrs. Stonum glanced around at the streets crowded with carriages and wagons heading across the river and away from the capital. She lowered her voice. "I heard it on good authority that President Davis has ordered his wife and children to leave for South Carolina."

Emily stopped walking and looked up sharply at the older woman. "That sounds as if Mr. Davis doesn't think the Union can be stopped!"

"Unfortunately, you're right. Girls, I think you should both consider leaving until this is over."

"Where would we go?" Hannah cried. "For weeks, people have been coming *here* to escape the Yankees coming up the peninsula! Now they're leaving. Where would we be safe?"

"I don't know," Mrs. Stonum admitted, starting to walk again. "But almost anywhere away from the capital. The Yankees are determined to seize Richmond in hopes of ending the war."

Emily understood that Richmond was not only the seat of the Confederate government but was also home to the South's only major armament factory. Richmond represented the very heart of the struggling new breakaway nation. Seize the heart, and the Confederacy would die.

Emily asked somberly, "Are you going, too?"

"No, I can't. You've already seen wounded men being brought in from the peninsula field hospitals. That's only a trickle of what will follow when major battles begin. Soon there won't be nearly enough surgeons or even nurses. My duty is to stay here and do what I can."

"Then I'm staying, too!" Emily declared firmly. "I'll never get my pass if I leave. Besides, I've learned enough from you that I could help in nursing if it gets really bad."

"I pray that I'm wrong," Mrs. Stonum said, "but I'm afraid it's going to get very bad before long."

Emily saw her chance to confront Hannah again. "What about you?" she asked.

Hannah shrugged. "I know how to make cartridges for our soldiers. I'll stay."

Emily had a sudden horrible thought of what a Union gunboat's shell would do if it struck the munitions factory where Hannah worked, south of town on an island in the James River. Quickly, Emily pushed through the conversational opening Mrs. Stonum had created. "But, Hannah, if something happened to either of us, I wouldn't want to have hard feelings between us. I'd like us to be friends again—real friends."

"You mean you'll tell me how you get Mr. Fitzhugh to deliver your letters for free?"

Emily hesitated, trying to tactfully refuse, but Mrs. Stonum spoke first.

"What's this?" she asked in surprise.

Hannah blurted, "He delivers Emily's mail even though she has no money to pay him—that's what!"

Mrs. Stonum stopped walking again to look straight into Emily's eyes. "Is this true?"

Emily felt trapped and a little frightened, not to mention upset over Hannah's remark. "Yes," Emily admitted, "but I can't talk about it."

Mrs. Stonum studied Emily in silence for a few seconds before saying, "Well, I don't mean to pry, but since neither of you girls has a mother to counsel you, I hope you won't mind if I speak my concern about this."

"Why?" Emily protested. "I haven't done anything wrong!"

"I didn't say you had," the widow replied gently, "and I assume it wasn't your idea to say nothing about this arrangement."

"That's right!" Hannah declared. "She didn't even mean to tell me, but she accidentally let it slip. Then she wouldn't say why! Make her tell, Mrs. Stonum."

"I can't do that, Hannah. But, Emily, I assume that since you have no money for mail, some sort of exchange has been made. Am I right?"

★ ★

Emily squirmed, not wanting to break her word to Mr. Fitzhugh, yet not wanting to cause tension between her and the woman who had been her benefactor all these months. "I can't say anything without breaking my word, so please don't ask me anything more."

Mrs. Stonum briefly closed her eyes, took a deep breath, and slowly let it out. "Very well." She opened her eyes and fixed them firmly on Emily. "I won't push you, but I want you to ask yourself this: Why would Mr. Fitzhugh not want you to tell what he must have asked you to do?"

"Right!" Hannah exclaimed. "Exactly my thoughts! Why? And what if that keeps you from getting your pass back to Illinois?"

Emily flinched as though she were slapped. She didn't see any possible connection, but she hadn't thought about that, either. And why did Fitzhugh want her to keep this secret?

The feeling of concern that she had experienced after he walked away with her first letters suddenly surged back. She resumed walking with Hannah and Mrs. Stonum, but the question pounded in her head.

*Why? What possible reason could he have for swearing me to secrecy?* Whatever it was, she had a sick feeling that somehow she had made a terrible mistake.

# TAXES AND TROUBLES

At midweek, Gideon and Fletcher stepped back to examine the finishing touches they had put on the room built in the barn. "There," Fletcher said with satisfaction. "That's about the best living quarters a man could ask for."

"It looks good," Gideon agreed. "After we sell our wheat crop, we should have enough cash to put in a stove before winter so you can keep warm."

"I won't need one. Remember, I told your mother and you that I'll move on after the crops are in this fall."

Gideon hadn't forgotten. In the weeks since Fletcher had been well enough to help around the farm, life had been easier on the boy. He still stewed about his mother and remarriage. Gideon hated to think of the misery he would suffer if Fletcher left and she married Cobb.

"You could stay on through the winter," Gideon said.

"Thanks, but when I've at least partly repaid your mother and the family for nursing me back to health, I'll return to the Shenandoah."

"There won't be much left, judging from what I hear the Yankees are doing, trying to catch General Jackson."

"I can start over. Maybe I can help beat the enemy, even if I'm not able to be in the army anymore."

"If the Yankees come here, you could help me fight them," Gideon said a little desperately.

★ ★

"I pray that doesn't happen, but if it does, don't fight them. Take your mother and family and get away."

"I'm not leaving this place!" Gideon declared firmly. "I hate it, but it's all we've got, and I'm not going to let Mama lose it, not even to William Lodge!"

"If your mother can't pay the taxes, the sheriff will seize this place and sell it."

Gideon remembered William's threat about that, but he had put it out of his mind. Now he realized that it was something he had to face. He asked Fletcher, "When are those due?"

"If your mother hasn't told you, maybe I'm speaking out of turn. Why don't you ask her?"

"Papa and Mama never discussed such things with me or in front of me, my brother, or my sisters. It's all right, you can tell me."

"I'd rather not say anything more, but if I had the money, I'd—"

"Thanks," Gideon broke in. "I've got to see Mama."

★ ★ ★ ★ ★

Emily made up her mind that when Fitzhugh came again, she would insist he tell her why she had to keep their arrangement a secret. She didn't have much time to brood about Fitzhugh or even to again try getting a pass.

The wounded began arriving in ever increasing numbers as General Joseph E. Johnston valiantly fought the Union hordes approaching Richmond, slowing their movement up the peninsula. The city hospitals were soon overflowing, so the wounded were laid in tents or moved into private homes.

Surgeons prohibited girls from trying to help nurse, so usually Emily's duties were limited. While Mrs. Stonum cared for the seriously wounded, Emily wrote letters home for ambulatory soldiers or read the Bible to them. She wanted to do more as the tide of incoming wounded increased; the sight of bloody young men in pain sickened her. Even though they were

★ ★

Confederates and she was a loyal Unionist, the wounded touched her heart.

One day outside a hospital tent, she impulsively picked up a pan of water and a cloth. She entered the tent, where several men were laid out in a row on pallets. Trying to control her emotions at the stench and the groans of pain, she averted her eyes from everything except the nearest man. She deliberately avoided looking at the bloody wounds in both of his arms and his right leg. His eyes were closed and his face so blackened by gunpowder that he was unrecognizable.

She knelt by his side and asked softly, "Would you like me to wash your face?"

His eyes slowly opened and tried to focus. "Sis?" he asked dreamily. "Where's Mama?"

"I'm Emily." It was difficult to keep her composure. "Your sister couldn't come. Your mother's all right." She silently prayed that she would be forgiven for telling such a lie, but she felt the soldier was out of his mind with pain and shock. "The water may be cold," she warned and gently began washing the blackened face.

There was pain in his eyes as they tried to focus on her face. "How bad am I hurt?" he asked weakly.

"You'll have to ask the surgeon." With each gentle wipe of the cloth, the soldier's white face slowly emerged. *Why, he's just about the same age as Brice!*

"I never saw an angel," the soldier said wistfully. "But if they're all as pretty as you, heaven must be a beautiful place."

The compliment flustered Emily. "Shh!" she said, not knowing what else to do. "Try to rest and get well."

A man on a stretcher next to him said, "Miss, he can go to heaven if he likes, but I want to stay here. How about checking me and telling me what my chances are?"

"I'm not a nurse," Emily replied without looking at him. She gently dried her patient's face and noticed he didn't even

★ ★

have any sign of a beard. "There," she said. "You look much better."

He murmured his thanks as the second soldier again urged her to check him. She said she would wash his face and got up to replace the dirty basin of water.

The second soldier's voice stopped her. "Just take one look," he pleaded, his tone softening. "I can't see."

She turned toward him and almost dropped the pan. His eyes were gone from a horrible facial wound. An involuntary sob seized Emily. She spun away from the gruesome sight, closed her eyes tightly, and stood still, unable to speak or move.

"You!" A gruff voice made her eyes pop open. A surgeon stood in the opening to the tent and wiped a bloody scalpel on his soiled apron. "No girls allowed to nurse these men! Get out of here!"

Startled, Emily explained, "I was just—"

"Out! Out!" the surgeon cried. "I have enough trouble without some child bothering these men!"

Emily started to protest but realized the futility of that. She stumbled blindly out of the tent, feeling as if she had just been kicked in the heart.

★　★　★　★　★

Each day, Nat felt more confident of eluding slave catchers as he met more and more fugitives fleeing up the peninsula. Blacks and whites were so concerned with escaping the invaders that nobody paid any attention to him. Hunger became his main concern.

Most of the plantations he passed had been abandoned. He knew all able-bodied masters would either be fighting the Yankees or fleeing with what little could be saved. But still there might be an older white man or even a mistress who would recognize that his manner and clothing meant he was a runaway with a price on his head. He had to steer clear of this possibility.

So he walked on south, looking for a smaller house where a non-slaveholder might live. Most homes had the blinds down and a desolate, abandoned look about them. When it was obvious a home had been abandoned, he'd enter the gardens, orchards, and fields, searching for food.

Nat ate what little the invading armies had left, but it wasn't enough. He needed something more satisfying, so he kept alert for a stray chicken or a smokehouse where a ham might have been overlooked. But each place had been stripped as clean as if locusts had ravaged it.

He had hoped to come to a Union camp by now, but all he saw were blue-clad troops marching by day and their thousands of temporary campfires at night. There were no signs of a permanent encampment.

He came to a modest frame house where an old white woman with a cane hobbled toward the well curb, with a wooden bucket in her hand. After glancing around to make sure no one else was in sight, he approached her.

"Your pardon," he said with a slight bow and lowered eyes. No slave was allowed to look a white person in the eyes but was always to assume a humble and subservient attitude. "Please allow me to draw the water for you, Mistress."

She eyed him suspiciously from under a faded gray bonnet, then extended the bucket. "Those thieving Yankees took everything I got. Searched my bedchamber and left me with nothing but a few candle stubs. Even the chain to get water from my well. But I hid a rope."

He accepted the pail, thinking he had wasted his time. If the soldiers had taken everything, she might not even have enough for herself. But he had come this far off the road; he would wait and hope for some food.

She reached under her frayed apron and held out a coil of rope. "Here. Use this."

"Thank you." He carried rope and bucket to the well curb. Looking down, he saw the well was cool, deep, and smelled

★ ★

clean. Wordlessly, he attached the rope to the supporting half-loop of leather that served as a handle. He played out the rope, letting the bucket's weight carry it down until it splashed gently on the water's surface.

"I watched you coming down the road," the woman said. "How come you're headed south instead of north like the rest?"

He let the heavy bucket sink until it was full, then pulled it up by the rope, hand over hand, without looking at her. "I'm searching for a Yankee encampment."

"Why?" Suspicion sounded in her voice.

He lifted the bucket of water clear of the well, sloshing some over the top. "I heard my mother is working as a laundress in one of them."

"You're a runaway." It was a statement, but not accusatory.

He avoided a direct answer. "I'll carry this to the house for you," he said, motioning with his free hand for her to go ahead of him.

She shook her head and pointed with the cane for him to go first. "Body servant," she guessed, falling in behind him, "judging from the way you talk. Probably started as a yard boy, then moved into the big house."

He hadn't started the usual way, but he was too hungry to risk correcting her. "Yes, Mistress."

"I didn't think you people cared any more about your family than a bunch of puppies for their mother."

Anger instantly surged through Nat, but he had long ago learned to control his responses. "Mine's different."

"You don't say?" She sounded surprised and a little pleased. When he nodded, she said, "You hungry?"

He felt a rush of hope. She had outwitted the soldiers who stole her well chain; maybe she did have some food hidden away. "Yes, Mistress."

"You sit here on the back step," she said as they neared the house. "I've got some cool buttermilk and cornbread. Maybe even a bit of ham."

★ ★

She reached for the bucket, indicating she didn't want him to enter the house. He held the door open for her, then sat down, his stomach constricting painfully at the prospect of good food.

When she returned with a plate, a glass, and flatware, she asked, "Are you wondering why I'm here all alone?"

He wasn't, but he nodded and took the offering.

She swung the cane in a wide, sweeping half-circle. "I was born and married here. Birthed four children. All dead. Buried my husband over there." The cane stopped momentarily. "I'll die here. No Yankee dogs are going to run me off."

Nat tried not to gulp, but he couldn't resist quickly swallowing several ounces of buttermilk and taking a big bite of the ham. He chewed quickly, then tensed, his eyes flickering toward a grove of trees.

The old woman asked, "You sure you're looking for your mammy?"

"Yes, Mistress." He stopped chewing. A small group of blue-coated horsemen trotted out of the woods and into the open field, heading for the back of the house.

"There's a Yankee camp about two miles west of here," she said, obviously unaware of the cavalrymen. "I saw countless pieces of laundry on the line the last time I went to church that way. Soldier boys don't do more than wash their socks and underdrawers when they have to, so there must be a black woman or two doing . . ."

As she caught sight of the soldiers, she left her sentence unfinished and shaded her eyes against the sun's glare. "You can't outrun their horses," she said quietly. "You may have to give up looking for your mammy for a while."

Alarmed and surprised, Nat set the now empty plate down on the step beside him. "They aren't slave catchers. They don't want me. I heard they protect people like me."

"Mostly they do, but I recognize that big heavyset rider in front. He's the sergeant who led his men in here and took the

★ ★

last chickens I had. Rode off with their feet tied across the sad-dles and much clucking and flapping of wings."

Nat stood up, ready to run, but the woman shook her head. "Yankees pay wages to what they call contraband, meaning runaway slaves that come into their lines, but then they work them just like their old masters did."

Nat suddenly turned and ran around the side of the house, but wild shouts from the approaching horsemen warned that he had been seen. He heard the drumming of their horses' hooves on the ground.

He kept running, but he knew the old woman was right. He wasn't going to see his mother anytime soon.

★ ★ ★ ★ ★

Gideon hated to see his mother cry. She dropped wearily into her old hickory rocker and threw her apron over her face. Gideon dropped on his knees beside her and wrapped his arms around her shoulders.

"Please don't cry, Mama!" he pleaded, fighting to keep his own tears in check. "We'll find a way!"

"I've prayed so hard!" Her voice was muffled by the apron. "I didn't want to tell you because there was nothing you could do about the taxes. Besides, you've already got more burdens than you should have to bear."

"Then how come you told Mr. Fletcher?"

"I didn't." She dropped the apron to look at her son with teary eyes. "He guessed, saying he knew that his own property taxes would be due if he still owned a farm in the Shenandoah. I couldn't lie to him."

Gideon nodded and stood up. "How long do we have?"

"They're due July first but won't be delinquent until No-vember. If they're not paid by then, the law makes the sheriff take the farm to be sold for taxes and late penalties."

"So," Gideon said, "if that happens, then I guess the sheriff

★ ★

will sell our place, William can pay the taxes plus penalties, and this will become his?"

"Yes, but we still have a little time. . . ."

He didn't hear the rest. He walked to the window and looked out.. His little sisters were playing in the yard, but he didn't really notice them. He told his mother, "Last year the summer wheat wasn't ready until mid-July, but Mr. Fletcher thinks this year we can harvest in late June. If so, maybe it'll bring enough money for taxes."

"We need more than just enough to pay the taxes. We also need money for things we can't grow or make. The big problem is getting any crop to market. The Yankees are roaming up and down the Shenandoah Valley trying to catch General Jackson, and the Union is threatening Manassas. So that leaves only Richmond, and that's a far piece, especially with the Yankees closing in on it the way they are. It could fall before the crop is ready."

Gideon turned to look at her. She had a sad, faraway look. "What're you thinking?" he asked. When she didn't reply, suddenly, he knew. "No, Mama! No! Forget Barley Cobb! There's got to be another way!"

"He's not rich, but he's always got money."

"Yes! For catching slaves after his dogs chew them up! He's a terrible, terrible person! Don't even think of it! We'll find another way to—!" He broke off as the hounds suddenly barked from the back porch and started running around the house toward the lane.

Mrs. Tugwell jumped up. "Somebody's coming! I can't be seen looking like this! Go see who it is while I fix myself up a little!"

Gideon started for the kitchen door, but it burst open and Kate rushed in. "He's coming!" she cried. "He's coming!"

"Who?" Gideon asked.

"Barley Cobb!"

★ ★

# THE STRUGGLE
# WITHIN

Gideon had thought Cobb would never show his face around the Tugwell farm again after Gideon's mother ordered him off the property on his last visit. Now he sat in the kitchen as though nothing had happened.

Gideon started to leave, but his mother asked him to stay. She was actually smiling at the untidy man. "What brings you here today, Mr. Cobb?" she asked.

Gideon watched him shift the ever present wad of chewing tobacco from his right to left cheek before he answered. "Martha, I tell ye plain-out that my feelin's was bad hurt when I last seen ye."

"I'm sorry you feel that way," she replied, "but I had repeatedly asked you to say no more on the subject you obviously had in mind that night."

"To tell ye the bonded truth, Martha, I had to do some tall thinkin' to fergive ye for what ye done. But I'm too kindhearted to hold a grudge, so I come to tell ye I fergive ye."

Gideon caught a flash of outrage in his mother's eyes before she said coolly, "I don't remember asking your forgiveness."

The slave catcher replied through his tobacco-stained brown beard, "Don't matter none. The Good Book says ye got to fergive, so I done that whether ye asked or not. Now, that settled, lemme tell ye why I come."

Gideon didn't want to hear what Cobb had to say, so he

stood up from where he had been sitting on a bench at the kitchen table. "I have to go help Mr. Fletcher."

"Fletcher?" Cobb repeated, his voice suddenly hard. "Is that the name of that thar feller who was leechin' off'n ye when I was here the last time?"

"He was a sick, wounded soldier in need of care," she replied quietly. "We did what we could for him."

"He's had plenty o' time to git well!" Cobb rose from the chair that had been Gideon's father's. "Ye ought to done sent him packin' long ago."

"Mr. Cobb!" Gideon's mother exclaimed sharply. "I do not need you to tell me what my Christian duty is!"

The slave catcher shook his head. His shoulder-length dark brown hair flopped around the sides of his head. "Martha, it's plain that ye ain't got the sense of a goose! Ye need somebody to—"

"Good-bye, Mr. Cobb!" she interrupted. "Gideon, please go with Mr. Cobb to his mule and watch him until he leaves this property!"

"Now, lookee here, Martha!" Cobb protested. "That ain't no way to talk to a man who kin he'p ye—"

"Gideon, the door! Quickly!" his mother cried.

He hurried over to open it, aware that he was so angry at the insult just thrown at his mother that he wanted to kick the departing guest in his backside. Gideon fought back his impulse. "Better leave!" he cried, his voice breaking. "And don't ever come back!"

Cobb strode to the door, his small hazel eyes blazing under heavy eyebrows. Those eyes reminded Gideon of a mean boar hog.

"Now ye done it, Martha!" Cobb raged. "Ye lost yore last chance! Ye'll live to regret it! Yore kids, too!"

★ ★ ★ ★ ★

The lieutenant leading the cavalry patrol that had captured

★ ★

Nat briefly questioned him. The officer turned to a boyish-look-ing trooper. "Clemmons, give him a hand so he can ride behind you back to camp."

"Ah, Lieutenant, I don't want his kind—"

"You heard me!" the officer said sharply. "Move!"

In obvious reluctance, Clemmons moved his mount up in front of Nat and reached down to him. Nat swung up behind the saddle and automatically started to extend his arms around the soldier's waist to hang on.

"Don't you dare!" the soldier snapped, twisting in the sad-dle to glare at Nat. "You grab on to the saddle the best you can and hold on. If you slide off, I hope my horse steps on your black face!"

Nat rankled at that remark, but he had learned long ago to hide his feelings from white folks. He managed to get a pre-carious finger grip on the cantle at the back of the open Mc-Clellan saddle seat.

As the trooper began riding, Clemmons said over his shoul-der, "You're soon going to be free. Not that I'm in favor of let-ting you people go, but rumor has it that President Lincoln is about to officially free all slaves in states now in rebellion. This war's no longer about keeping the Union together, but about your people."

Nat knew it didn't matter that his father was white, because the law said that children born of slave mothers were also slaves. Nat said nothing, but concentrated on keeping his seat.

"So, boy," the soldier continued, "your former master can't touch you here, but until you and all your race is free, you'll work. The Union will pay, feed, and house you, so probably for the first time, you'll be treated like a human being instead of what you are."

Nat silently ground his teeth. His concern was for his mother and sister, so he tried to change the subject. He asked, "Do you have some laundry women in your camp?"

Instead of answering, Clemmons twisted his head around

★ ★

and looked at Nat. "Where did you learn to speak good English?"

"My first master taught me."

"I thought that was against the law in this state."

"It is, but some masters or mistresses taught a few of us to become literate."

"Very few, I'd guess." Clemmons' tone softened slightly. "You're the first one I've ever heard that I could understand. Say, you know what? You being able to read and write, maybe the major will let you help his orderly. Otherwise, the sergeant will put you to pushing a wheelbarrow or digging latrines."

Instead of answering, Nat repeated his question about black laundresses.

"Oh, sure," Clemmons said. "Every camp has some. Why do you ask?"

"I'm looking for a certain woman. I was told she's washing clothes in one of the Federal camps. She has a little girl with her."

"Lots of black women are in these camps, some with little ones."

Greatly encouraged, Nat arrived at the white Union camp, where several black men were busy at menial chores. Nat did not see any women. Still, he was hopeful as the cavalrymen reined in before a line of picketed horses. A big blond sergeant walked toward the new arrivals.

As Nat started to slide off his mount, the soldier who let him ride behind him lowered his voice. "I don't like you or your kind, but here comes a man I dislike more. Sergeant Kretzschmar is a Dutchman who hates you people even more than the rest of us. Don't cross him."

After the cavalrymen briefly explained how they had found Nat, the sergeant handed him a shovel and a broom. "Vell," he said with a heavy German accent, "earn your keep, boy." He scowled and pointed to the line of tethered animals. "Clean this place, and fast."

★ ★

Aware of Clemmons' warning, Nat took the shovel and broom and approached the horses. At least he was safe from William, and maybe his mother and sister might even be in this very camp. Suddenly, he stopped, seeing some tents in the distance with clothes hung out to dry. He thought that must be the laundry area. Maybe his mother and sister were there.

He tensed at the sound of someone running up behind him. He glanced around just as Sergeant Kretzschmar delivered a hard kick with his heavy boots. *"Achtung!"* he yelled as Nat dropped the broom and shovel and threw out his hands to break his fall. "When I say fast, you listen, *dumbkoff*!"

Nat scrambled up from the smelly mess where he had fallen. *Federals don't like black people any more than our old masters did*, Nat thought bitterly. He added to himself, *Welcome to Yankee freedom!*

★ ★ ★ ★ ★

Over the next several days, Gideon silently fretted about the danger of losing the farm to tax problems, yet he didn't feel comfortable mentioning them to Fletcher. Instead, as they repaired a snake fence in a far corner of the river bottom near Black Water Swamp, Gideon asked, "Do you think the Yankees are really going to be able to take Richmond?"

Fletcher dropped his hammer and brushed away the clouds of mosquitoes that flew in from the adjacent swamp. "When I was a soldier, the generals didn't tell me anything. Yet almost everyone else in camp figured that after the whupping we gave the Yankees last year at Manassas, they learned that they can't take the capital that way. So they switched to the peninsula and are now closing in fast on the capital by land and the river. Truthfully, Gideon, the Yankees are going to be difficult to stop. But General Joe Johnston is giving them quite a fight."

"I have a friend named Emily in Richmond. Do you think she's in danger?"

"I hope not, but from what I've heard in the village or read

★ ★

in newspapers I picked up after they had been thrown away, General McClellan has around a hundred thousand Union men moving overland toward Richmond. We have less than half that number. The only advantage I can see is that McClellan is very cautious. It's taken him two months to move the sixty miles to near Richmond."

Gideon picked up a rough fence board and laid it in place. He had heard that McClellan had moved his huge Army of the Potomac from Alexandria, Virginia, to Fort Monroe on the peninsula to try a new attack on Richmond.

That great mass of men and war materials had finally taken Yorktown, sixty miles away, then Williamsburg, just fifty-one miles away. It wasn't known for sure how much closer the Federals were to the capital, but they were certainly gaining ground.

Fletcher asked, "Emily? Is she the one your sisters tease you about because she sends you letters?"

Gideon lowered his eyes. "Emily and I are just friends."

"Good friends care about each other," Fletcher observed. "Have you written her?"

"Yes, finally, after I had money from my newspaper column to pay Mr. Fitzhugh to deliver them. But in one of her letters she asked a question I can't answer."

"What kind of question?"

Gideon hesitated before answering. "She wants to know what I think of Negroes and slavery."

"That should be easy to answer. Everyone has an opinion on that, so just tell her what you think."

"Well, a year or so ago I decided that it's not race, color, or background that determines a person's value, but what that person is like inside. But that's not the same as how I *feel* about black people and slavery." Gideon paused, then asked, "What do you think?"

Wrinkling his brow, Fletcher replied thoughtfully, "In the months I was laid up with this wound, I had time to read the books Mrs. Yates loaned us. I also did lots of thinking. You ever hear of William Wilberforce?"

Gideon shook his head. "Don't think so."

"He was a British statesman who died about thirty years ago. In 1807 he helped pass a bill abolishing the slave trade in England. That was over fifty years ago, but it was only last month that Lincoln signed the bill that abolished slavery in Washington, D.C."

As Fletcher secured the board into the fence, Gideon asked, "Do you think that's why the British ended slavery without having a war over it?"

"I'm sure it helped. I never owned slaves, and your mother tells me your father never did. Fact is, most landowners in the South don't own slaves. But the rich men own the slaves and also control the politics."

"Is that why I've heard some people say that this is a 'rich man's war but a poor man's fight'?"

"I reckon. But to answer Emily's question, you have to look inside yourself about your thoughts on black people and slavery."

"Once I told her that slavery seemed natural," he admitted. "Of all the people I know, only two are against slavery." He glanced around, but there wasn't another person anywhere in sight. Still, Gideon lowered his voice to a confidential level.

"They're Mr. and Mrs. Yates, who own the *Church Creek Villager*, where my column runs. They also do some farming, but they freed their slaves. They hired some back on wages. The Yateses are thought to be abolitionists. Anyway, I have mixed feelings about slavery."

"How so?"

"Well, last year William Lodge got me kicked out of the little plantation school, before it closed when the war started. Anyway, after that, a slave boy who could read and write taught me to read better. He was just like me in all ways except he was part black." Gideon paused before adding thoughtfully, "And

★ ★

I'm free and he's not. Well, he might be now because he ran away and hasn't been caught, as far as I know."

"You speaking of one of your neighbor's people?"

*People?* Nat silently repeated. Fletcher hadn't used the usual word, 'slave,' or worse. "Yes," Gideon said. "His name is Nat. He risked a whipping every time he slipped away from his owner, William Lodge, to help me in what he called a 'pit school.' Why would he do that?"

"Sounds to me as though he's got a good heart."

"But he's a slave!" Gideon found himself getting worked up. "Slaves are property, like a horse or dog or something. Even the United States Supreme Court said so before the war."

"You go to Sunday school and church," Fletcher pointed out. "Have you read what the Scriptures say about slavery?"

"No, but the preachers say the Scriptures approve of—"

"Some preachers, not all," Fletcher corrected. "Most of the time, churches call pastors who agree with them. Yet some denominations broke away over this very issue, so not all preachers see the Bible favoring slavery."

Gideon found himself getting tense, as though he was arguing a lost cause. He blurted, "Last year, Emily told me about a woman guest at Briarstone, where Emily was then living, who said that slavery was ordained of the Lord."

After pausing, Gideon added, "I remember because I wrote it down in my journal. Emily told me that this woman said something about how 'upwards of four million of the colored race have been brought from heathen Africa and rescued from the foulest of paganism.' That's what churches have done for slaves."

"While making them sit up in the balcony so close to the rafters with the heat, the wasps, and hornets, or making them meet at other times than white folks."

Gideon looked suspiciously at Fletcher. "Are you one of those abolitionists?"

"No, I'm not brave enough for that."

★ ★

"But you were brave enough to go to war and lose your hand!"

"It takes a different kind of bravery to fight against what people think, Gideon. I'd like to be that kind of man, but so far I'm not. I keep my thoughts to myself, except for telling you."

Frowning thoughtfully, Gideon asked, "Do you think God is against slavery?"

Fletcher motioned for Gideon to follow him. They moved to the shade of a nearby tree and sat down, their backs against the trunk.

"Gideon," the man began, "slavery is against God's plan for families. Starting with Adam and Eve, the Lord set people in families. His principle of keeping families together is violated when black children are sold off from their mothers, wives from husbands, and so forth."

Gideon was sorry he had started this discussion. It made him think of things he had never before considered, and these made him uncomfortable.

Fletcher added, "When next you read your Bible, find the verse that says God made all men of one blood."

Gideon stared in surprise. "Where does it say that?"

"The book of Acts, chapter seventeen, beginning with verse twenty-four. It says that God made the world and all things therein. Then in verse twenty-six it says He 'hath made of one blood all nations of men. . . .' "

Fletcher paused, then added, "One blood. If we believe the Bible, then that makes everyone, including black people, my brothers and sisters—and yours."

Gideon was stunned. He started to shake his head violently but stopped when the big bell began clanging from the house. Gideon started to glance at the sun but knew it wasn't time to go in to eat. The bell rang hard and fast.

★ ★

"That's the alarm signal!" Gideon cried, leaping up. "Something's happened!" He started running toward the house while the bell's urgent peals echoed across the land and faded into the adjacent swamp.

★ ★

# SECRETS AND SILENCE

Emily had collapsed wearily in the second-story bedroom of Mrs. Stonum's house. Taking off her shoes, she sat on the edge of her high bed and rubbed her feet, glad that Hannah wasn't home yet. She felt humiliated that the surgeon had rudely ordered her away from helping wounded men. She ached with loneliness, which sometimes happened when she was alone and things weren't going well. She missed her parents and brothers so very much. She also missed her best girl friend, Jessie, in Illinois.

*Careful!* Emily warned herself as tears began to form behind her eyelids. *Don't go feeling sorry for yourself. That won't help.*

At a knock on the front door, she slid off the high bed and, in stockinged feet, hurried to the window. A gig sat at the curb. Emily frowned, trying to remember why it looked familiar. Suddenly, she knew. *Mr. Fitzhugh!*

She heard the front door open and Mrs. Stonum's voice as Emily hastily pulled her shoes back on. She hoped he had a letter from Gideon. Most of all, she wanted to ask questions to ease her conscience about their secret arrangement.

Emily hurried down the stairs and into the parlor, where Fitzhugh and the widow were conversing. Emily's heart leaped at the sight of three unopened envelopes in the volunteer mailman's hands. She knew they must be for her because nobody ever wrote Hannah. But were they from her cousin Julie at Briarstone or from Gideon?

"Ah, good afternoon, Emily!" Fitzhugh greeted her heartily. "I brought you something." He extended the three letters toward her.

"Thank you." She glanced down and recognized Gideon's scrawled handwriting on two envelopes. The small, neat penmanship on the third was clearly Julie's.

Mrs. Stonum said, "Please excuse me a moment, Mr. Fitzhugh, I'm going to make some coffee. Well, it's not real coffee because of the Yankee blockade, but at least it will be warm and comforting while we talk."

"Of course," the slender, well-dressed guest replied. "Emily and I can visit until you return."

Emily realized that she should have volunteered to make the coffee so she could also quickly read her letters, but she must talk to Fitzhugh alone. She invited him to sit down on the large, circular Victorian sofa.

As he settled against the central column that served as a backrest, Emily sat in the spindle-back Boston rocker. She glanced around to make sure Mrs. Stonum was out of earshot, planning to immediately discuss her concerns that Hannah's curiosity had raised.

But Fitzhugh spoke first. "In the brief moments Mrs. Stonum and I had before you came downstairs," he began in a low voice, "she mentioned that you help her with wounded soldiers. What do you do for them?"

Emily hurriedly explained, so she could bring up her questions. "The surgeons won't let girls do real nursing, so I do what some others my age are allowed to do: read to the wounded, sing, write letters. . . ."

"Do you talk with them?"

"Sometimes those who are less seriously hurt want to talk. They've been through such awful experiences, seeing their friends killed before their eyes and then getting hit themselves.

★ ★

They seem to want to tell me about it, though it upsets me to listen. Of course, I don't let them see that."

"I suppose most of them are being brought in from the fighting on the peninsula?"

"Yes, of course."

"Do you ask where they were when they were wounded? How many men are in their camps and that sort of thing?"

"Sometimes, but . . ." Emily let her words trail off as she glanced toward the kitchen. "Mr. Fitzhugh, before Mrs. Stonum comes back in here, there's something I have to ask."

"It sounds serious," he replied, leaning toward her. "What is it?"

"I accidentally let slip to my roommate that you delivered mail for me. She wanted to know where I got the money. Of course, I wouldn't tell her, but she indicated that she intended to keep prying until I told her. So I got to wondering: Why did you make me promise to keep our arrangement secret?"

"My dear Miss Emily," he said, leaning back and smiling disarmingly, "you surprise me. We discussed that at the time. It wouldn't be fair to Mrs. Stonum and others for me to do that for you and not charge—"

"I know!" she interrupted. "But you also asked me to let you know what I see and hear from the soldiers—"

"I explained that, too!" he broke in. Then, more quietly, "People expect me to know little bits of information, which I share with others whom I serve on my route. That's what I'll do here when Mrs. Stonum returns. You're doing many people a service. Now, please don't give it another thought. Here she comes with our coffee. Let's say no more about this, and I'll fill you in on what's going on with your cousins and the Tugwells."

Emily was disappointed that she hadn't been able to discuss her concerns more, but what he said seemed logical. She nodded and rose to help Mrs. Stonum serve, but Emily was still dissatisfied. She expected to feel better when she read the letters from Gideon and Julie.

★ ★

★ ★ ★ ★ ★

Gideon outran John Fletcher, whose recent illness had weakened and slowed him. Out of breath and frightened by the way the family alarm bell had been beaten so hard, Gideon saw with relief that the house wasn't on fire. His mother wasn't sprawled on the ground. Ben wasn't in sight, but both little sisters were running toward him. Kate was several yards in front of little Lilly, who vainly cried for her to wait.

"What's the matter?" Gideon yelled, sucking great gulps of air into his tortured lungs. "Where's Ben?"

"He's coming." Kate pointed off to the left.

Gideon glanced that way and saw his little brother running hard toward the house with the two hounds bounding ahead of him. "Is Mama hurt?" Gideon asked, turning back to Kate.

"No, it's Mrs. Yates." Kate slowed enough to turn and point back without stumbling. "She's waiting inside with Mama."

"What happened?" he asked, feeling relieved that his family was okay.

"The Yates's little neighbor girl is lost in the swamp, and Mrs. Yates needs you to take the hounds and find her before it's too late."

Any relief that Gideon had started to feel suddenly vanished. Black Water Swamp was a vast, forbidden area filled with several kinds of poisonous snakes, black bears, wild horned cattle, and other large animals. Some people claimed they had heard panthers screaming deep within the wasteland of stinking mud, tangled brush, and dense towering forests that had never been successfully logged.

Even the sun could not penetrate its dark, unknown, and mysterious heart. Countless scary stories were told in hushed tones about runaway slaves and even white men who had ventured into the area and never been seen again.

Gideon tried to control his breathing so he could talk better. "Whose little girl?" he asked Kate.

★ ★

Kate answered as John Fletcher reached them. "Her name's Cassie, but I didn't hear her last name. Mrs. Yates said her folks live on the other side of the swamp near some land Mr. Yates farms. That's all I heard before Mama made me go ring the bell."

Kate turned back around, saying, "Come on!" She sprinted toward the house, passing her little sister, who wept and wearily plopped down in the dust.

Gideon reached down as he dashed by. He quickly helped her to her feet and took her right hand in his left. "It's all right," he assured Lilly. "I'll help you."

"I'll help, too," Fletcher said, catching up to them on Lilly's left side. He gripped her left hand in his right and urged, "Let's see if we can catch up to Kate."

Lilly stopped crying, apparently feeling better but still not understanding the situation. In moments, she suddenly started singing "Dixie" at the top of her voice and continued into the house.

★ ★ ★ ★ ★

When Nat finally was allowed to put his shovel and broom away, his hands were blistered and bleeding. He washed up at the nearest horse trough. The water stung his fresh sores, but the manual labor had also made his unaccustomed shoulder and arm muscles very tender. He closed his eyes and moaned softly when bending over the trough to gently wash his face.

A voice said quietly, "Ain't no use tryin' to please Sergeant Kretzschmar. He don't like the color of our skin."

Nat stopped washing, rubbed the water off his eyes, and turned to see the speaker. He was about Nat's age but had thick biceps and a neck that looked as big around as Nat's chest. Muscles rippled like living things under the black skin.

"They call me Mingo," he continued as he poised over the water, his massive hands cupped to dip into it. "You just come through the lines?"

★ ★

Nat saw no reason to try explaining that he had escaped to Canada and deliberately returned to Virginia. "I'm Nat," he said, adding, "Yes, just got here. You?"

"Escaped from my old master the day the Yankees landed on this peninsula. Say, you speak pretty good; not like most of our folks."

"I was thinking the same about you," Nat admitted. "How'd you learn to do that? From a benevolent master?"

"Taught myself, listenin' to the mistress, mostly. You?"

"I was fortunate. My first master believed in having his servants become literate. Many didn't want to, but I did."

"I see by your hands that you must have been a house servant."

"Body servant. I didn't know how soft I was until today."

"You'll harden up, but there ain't no pleasin' that Dutch sergeant. One day I heard the major ask him how come he enrolled to fight for the Yankees. He said there are thousands of German soldiers who serve the Union.

"Then the major said he knew lots of Irishmen who had joined up, too. Seems most of their parents fled Ireland because of a potato famine. Anyway, Kretzschmar told the major that he and most Germans were actually Americans, born of parents who had come from the old country."

"Why do they call them 'Dutch' instead of Germans?"

"I think it has something to do with the way they say the name of their own country. Sounds like 'Dutchland' or something. The sergeant was bragging to the major about what strict disciplinarians Germans are. He said that in the old country, they had a long and proud military heritage. That's why they're mighty good soldiers."

Nat forced himself to wash in spite of his sore hands and aching muscles. Drying himself on an old cloth that hung at the end of the trough, he said, "When they brought me in I saw lots of clothes drying over there." He motioned with his head

★ ★

toward the place where the laundry had been removed. "You ever been over there?"

"Have I?" Mingo laughed, winked, and playfully jabbed Nat in the ribs with his elbow. "They're washerwomen, black like us, who ran away when the Yankees came. Most are just plain old mammies, but a few are our age. I sneak over sometimes after lights-out to see a couple of the pretty ones. You want to come along some night?"

"Right now I just want to lie down and let these muscles relax a little. But I'll go with you sometime."

"Just one problem," Mingo cautioned. "If Kretzschmar sees us, he'll lay his pick handle on us hard enough to break bones. Then he'll set us to digging latrines the rest of the war. You still game?"

Nat thought of his mother and sister and nodded. "Just tell me when."

"Good! Just be ready when I come for you."

"I'll be ready," Nat replied. His aching hands and body didn't seem to hurt so much as his hopes rose.

★ ★ ★ ★ ★

The short, elderly publisher of the local village newspaper briefly explained the facts to Gideon, Ben, Kate, Lilly, and John Fletcher. "Cassie Yates was working with her father on their farm near the swamp when somehow she wandered off early this morning. Her father, Horatio, frantically searched for her for over an hour before he realized he was going to need help. He ran to our house. My husband went to help look and I rode here for you, Gideon. Will you come with your hounds?"

"Yates?" he repeated. "Your relatives?"

"No. Horatio is one of the slaves we freed. He took our surname when he started farming on his own."

*So the lost girl is black!* Gideon thought.

Gideon glanced at his mother. Her face was drawn and pale, and she had twisted the end of her apron into a tight ball.

"I would never consider it, Gideon," she said softly, "but Mrs. Yates reminded me that there's no one else around who has hunted that swamp as much as you and your father have. And you do have the hounds."

"But you know they're just plain old dogs who're trained only to follow a game scent," Gideon explained. "Just something we can eat. Rock and Red weren't taught to track a person. A coon, possum, or rabbit, yes. But I'm not sure what good they'd be in finding a lost little girl."

Gideon shook his head. "They'd almost certainly be no good. But what about Barley Cobb's hounds? They're trained to trail people."

"You mean runaway slaves," Mrs. Yates replied bitterly. "He boasts that's *all* his dogs will hunt. When they catch a black fugitive, the hounds tear him up terribly before Cobb gets to them. No, Gideon, we cannot use Barley Cobb's dogs. Maybe your hounds weren't trained to hunt people, but they may still be of some use to those men out there in that swamp!"

Gideon hesitated. It was easy to see that his mother didn't want him to go. Yet she obviously felt the agony that the parents of the lost girl must be going through. But what if something bad happened to him? How would his mother, brother, and sisters survive?

He wanted to ask his mother what to do, but he was old enough to realize that her silence meant it was his decision. The idea of entering the swamp frightened him. He and his father had often followed the hounds into the spooky underbrush, through peat moss and sucking mud. That was something few hunters dared to do. Gideon hadn't exactly been afraid with his father, a gun, and the hounds along, but he had stayed away since his father died.

What if he got lost? What if he was bitten by a rattlesnake, cottonmouth, or copperhead? There were unconfirmed reports of quicksand that could suck a full-grown man down where his

★ ★

body would never be found. What if he walked into one of these treacherous deathtraps?

Mrs. Yates looked somberly at him through her wire-rimmed glasses. Her deep blue eyes were tender as she said in a low voice, "I'll understand if you can't do it. You have your mother and siblings to think about."

Gideon still hesitated. He looked up at John Fletcher. His face showed deep concern, but he didn't say anything. Gideon understood that Fletcher felt he had no right to express an opinion. This was all up to Gideon.

He turned back to Mrs. Yates. "What happens if she's not found soon?"

She didn't answer right away, which caused Gideon to look up at her. Her usual wrinkle-free face seemed to have abruptly developed deep lines around her eyes. Gideon suspected she was trying not to weep.

Finally she said, "You know the answer to that."

Gideon nodded; he knew. The little girl could not survive long. He glanced at his baby sister and imagined what it would be like if she were out there, frightened and alone, vainly calling for someone who never came.

Slowly, Gideon straightened and looked first at his mother, then at Mrs. Yates. "I'll get the dogs," he said.

Over the relieved sigh from Mrs. Yates, Fletcher said quickly, "I'll go with you, Gideon."

★ ★

# A SURPRISE
# DEMAND

Emily and Mrs. Stonum rode a rented hack to the eastern end of Richmond's Broad Street, past Bloody Gulch and the sprawling Chimborazo Hospital on the high ground beyond. Some three thousand beds were already full of wounded in the complex of separate small buildings.

"As you know, Hannah is angry with me because I can't reveal why Mr. Fitzhugh is carrying my letters," Emily said. "Now I believe you're also upset with me."

"I'm not upset, Emily, but I am concerned."

"Please don't be. I don't want you to be unhappy with me. I talked to him and am confident it's all right. However, I can't tell you the details, because he made me promise to keep our letter-carrying agreement secret."

"What do you know about his loyalty to the South?"

"Loyalty?" The question surprised Emily. She thought back. "Well, the first time I saw him was when I arrived at church with my aunt and cousin Julie. Mr. Fitzhugh brought us the news that Union forces had surrendered at Fort Sumter. As I recall, he said it was 'a great victory.' Then he said something about 'that tyrant in Washington,' meaning Mr. Lincoln. That shocked me."

Mrs. Stonum lowered her voice and glanced at the back of the hack driver. "I keep telling you to be very careful in what you say about your views."

"I'm not trying to hide anything. Everyone knows where I stand and that I want to get home to Illinois."

Shaking her head, Mrs. Stonum warned, "Sometimes I wonder if your tendency to be outspoken in favor of the Union might be contributing to the delay in your pass."

"Why? Would you have me lie—even if I could?"

"No, of course not, but if you want that pass, remember that in a war, discretion is a good idea."

The hack pulled over to let several approaching ragged, weary, and barefooted Confederate soldiers pass from the opposite direction. Turning to his passengers, the driver observed, "They don't look in very good shape to hold the Yankees camped outside Richmond."

"They'll hold," Mrs. Stonum declared firmly. "If this city falls, the war is lost, and our boys know it. This is their homeland; they'll hold."

"I sure hope you're right," the driver said.

Emily wasn't so sure. For some time, the city had been filled with Virginians fleeing up the peninsula toward Richmond. Even the Confederate Congress and President Davis's wife had fled, indicating that those in high places doubted the city could be saved from the invading hordes. Enemy cannon fire could be heard outside the city. On the James River, the heavy boom of Union gunboats added to the sense of uncertainty.

After the last soldier passed and the hack moved on, Emily turned again to Mrs. Stonum. "I never say anything against the South, although I oppose slavery and I believe Mr. Lincoln is right to hold the Union together."

"I think it would be wise for you not to say that."

Emily was indignant. "I have to say what I believe!"

"Yes, that seems to be part of your nature. But please be careful."

"I will," Emily replied, "but I'll sure be glad when I get my pass so I can get home to my friend Jessie."

★ ★

"Have you heard from her lately?"

Emily sighed. "Not a word. But my cousin Julie at Briarstone wrote to say she wished I'd come back there."

"I assume you're not planning on doing that?"

"No. I'm going to Jessie's in Illinois."

"Have you heard from her brother?"

"Nothing from him, either; not since the last time I told you about." She lapsed into silence, a slight frown wrinkling her brow. *Where is Brice? I hope he's safe*. Her mind jumped. *What about Gideon? I wonder what he's doing.*

★ ★ ★ ★ ★

Horatio, the distraught freedman, was a tall, wiry farmer, who quickly led Gideon, Fletcher, and the hounds to the fringe of Black Water Swamp. He pointed to where he had last seen his little girl. Her barefoot tracks were barely visible along a corduroy road that began at the edge of the swamp and vanished in the dense undergrowth.

From his late father, Gideon had learned that the road had been made years ago by slaves. They laid logs crossways in the muck to build it above the water. Masters had vainly hoped to drain enough of the marsh to get at the valuable timber in the interior. The road was planned to give easier access to low areas that were to be drained by building canals. These didn't work, so commercial efforts had been halted, and the swamp remained somewhat primitive.

Men seldom ever ventured into the area, which was home to larger animals like white-tailed deer, bear, and wild cattle. There were also many smaller mammals and reptiles, as well as waterfowl and countless songbirds.

"She probably stuck to the road as long as possible," Gideon observed, "but she must have wandered off of it or else she would have followed it back here."

"Makes sense," Fletcher agreed.

The hounds strained so hard to be free of their short chains that they made choking sounds from where their leather collars cut into their throats. "Ready?" Gideon asked, turning to look at Fletcher, who had the search party's only weapon.

With just one hand, Fletcher couldn't fire the ten-pound, .69-caliber smooth bore flintlock musket that had belonged to Gideon's father. Gideon would have to take the weapon if it became necessary to use it against a bear or some other large animal. Fletcher tucked the nearly five-foot long musket under his right armpit and supported it with his hand. Slaves weren't allowed to own weapons, and even though Horatio was free, he didn't dare risk carrying a gun.

Fletcher glanced at Horatio, who handed the boy a muddy yellow dress Cassie had worn that morning. Cassie's father said she had dirtied it making mud pies. Her mother had changed her into a blue one shortly before she vanished. Gideon held it close to the dogs' noses, then forced their muzzles close to the girl's tracks. Rock's black-and-tan breed had been trained for centuries to follow animal scent. Red was a mixture of breeds including the bloodhound, whose ancestors had been taught to trail humans. But Red had only hunted game.

Gideon silently prayed the dogs would understand that he wanted them to follow Cassie's scent. "Seek!" Gideon urged firmly. "Seek! Seek!"

The dogs looked at him and whined at a command they had never heard before. He unsnapped their chains, and they bounded down the log road into the swamp.

Fletcher lowered his voice so that Horatio, standing a few feet away, could not overhear. "Gideon, do you think they're really going to follow her trail?"

Gideon didn't want to admit that he didn't really know the answer. He looked at the patched and faded yellow dress.

"I hope so," Gideon told Fletcher, watching the hounds running around, long ears flapping, cutting back and forth and sniffing noisily in their usual way.

Red, the "strike dog," suddenly bawled loudly and began

★ ★

running on the corduroy road into the dark swamp.

Horatio looked expectantly at Gideon, who saw the deep pain mixed with sudden hope in the father's dark eyes.

"They're on to something," Gideon said, hoping he wasn't misleading him. "See how Rock is joining in? Come on, but let's stay together."

They followed the short log road to where it ended. The solidness of logs gave way to soft, wet, spongelike peat. Mr. Tugwell had told Gideon that the dark brown mass was several feet deep and composed of twigs, leaves, rooted stumps, fallen logs, and other decaying organic material.

"Let's call for her," Gideon suggested, struggling to stand upright on the peat that sank beneath his feet.

Horatio nodded, cupped his hands, and called mightily, "Cassie! It's your papa! Can you hear me?"

They all stopped and waited, ears alert, but there was no answer.

"Try again," Gideon suggested quietly.

They did, but the results were the same.

Gideon again followed the sound of the hounds. In a few minutes, the swamp completely engulfed them. The sun was quickly blocked by a great canopy of trees, mostly red maple and black gum.

*We don't have much more time*, Gideon warned himself. *There's no way I can lead us out if I can't see the landmarks. We've got to find her and be out of the swamp before sunset.*

Pushing aside trailing vines and saplings that had grown across the way, Gideon could see nothing except trees. He didn't remember it being so dark. It was strangely still except for the hounds' bawling fading into the swamp.

"What do you think?" he asked, turning to the men.

They bent to carefully search for the girl's tracks. There was a single barefoot print with a red smear on it. Gideon guessed she had cut herself or been scratched by some of the heavy

★ ★

brush. But there was nothing to indicate which way she had gone.

Fletcher leaned close to Gideon. "Your hounds went this way, but do you think they're really trailing her?"

Glancing at Horatio, Gideon whispered, "I wish I knew for sure." His eyes probed the undergrowth. "There!" he said, pointing. "A game trail. It's logical that the little girl would take the easiest way."

Horatio silently started toward the faint trail.

Gideon took the heavy musket from Fletcher. "I'll carry that for a while," he said and followed after Horatio. At once, the soggy peat sank under the boy's feet, making walking even more difficult. Fletcher brought up the rear.

Gideon hoped the hounds were really trailing the girl's scent and not following a coon or possum. But when he came to a short stretch of high ground, his sharp eyes spotted animal tracks heading away. Even while standing, he knew the larger ones had been made by his dogs. He bent to examine the second, and his heart sank.

*They're not following her! They're after a dumb old raccoon!*

★　★　★　★　★

Nat had wrapped his blistered and bleeding hands with an old cloth in a vain effort to ease the pain while he used the shovel and broom in the stables. Mingo began loading a wheelbarrow with the piles that Nat had made.

"I'm sorry you didn't find your mother and sister last night," he said.

"I didn't think it likely that I would find them right away," Nat replied. "But now all those laundry women know my mother's name and what she looks like. Same with Cordelia. If anyone comes in from another camp who's heard of either of them, they'll let me know."

"Even if you find them, then what?"

Nat didn't want to mention his plans to try smuggling his mother and sister to Canada by way of the Underground Railroad. He certainly didn't want to mention Edward Reverdy, the abolitionist in Richmond who had helped Nat escape to freedom.

Nat remembered what George, the old carriage driver at Briarstone, had told him before he ran away. *"Never trust anyone; not even our own kind. You never know who will betray you for a little trinket from white folks."*

"Right now," Nat replied evasively, "I'd just like to find them."

Mingo glanced toward Sergeant Kretzschmar. He had tucked a three-foot piece of pick handle under his armpit while he cursed another black fugitive for the way he was currying one of the Union's horses.

"I've known some mighty mean white men in my life, but that one's the worst," Mingo observed. "Sure, Lincoln's going to set us free, but what good's that if all Union men are like him?"

Nat kept busy, unwilling to risk letting the sergeant catch him stopping for a moment. In the short time he had been in the camp, Nat found that almost all of the Yankee soldiers treated him as an inferior.

"Seems about everybody hates anyone who's different," Nat mused. "When I was at my first master's, I heard the mistress tell her children about California's gold rush in '49. She said the white men who came from the East Coast put a tax on Mexicans and all other 'foreigners,' even though some had been there before the white men came."

"Why is it that white folks always seem to be the ones who decide who gets hated? White men came to Africa and stole our ancestors, brought them to this country against their wills, and made them slaves. Now we're in bondage. Why does our color make us the slave?"

"I don't know," Nat admitted.

★ ★

Mingo walked away, pushing the loaded wheelbarrow.

Nat stopped to fix the end of his hand bandage where it had come loose. He leaned the broom handle against his shoulder to free both hands.

"Caught you loafing!" Sergeant Kretzschmar's voice was so close behind him that Nat instinctively whirled around and defensively raised his hands.

"Raise your hand against me, vill you?" the sergeant yelled, his face turning red with anger. He snatched the pick handle from under his armpit and swung hard toward Nat's head.

★　★　★　★　★

Gideon was sick at heart knowing that a little girl might die all alone and frightened in the swamp because his hounds were on the wrong trail. Yet he couldn't bring himself to tell Horatio, who was eagerly pushing ahead through the tangled undergrowth, calling his daughter's name in a voice thick with emotion.

Breathing hard from the exertion of hurrying through the swamp, Gideon automatically checked for landmarks to help him find his way back. A lightning-blasted tree, a peculiarly shaped bush, and other objects that were slightly different imprinted themselves on his mind. After passing, he turned and viewed them so he would recognize each landmark from the opposite direction.

He raised his eyes beyond Horatio and caught a flash of light on water through the undergrowth. He recognized the location and pointed. "Up ahead there's a pond covering several acres, but some dry ridges are beyond that. She might head up there because the walking is easier."

The three searchers hurried as fast as the shaky peat would allow while they shouted and whistled. The swamp mocked them with silence. Even the hounds were now so far ahead that their voices were nearly lost in the vast shadowy world.

Gideon plunged ahead with the musket, passing Horatio.

★　★

The dogs had failed, yet Gideon couldn't really condemn them. They were not trained to trail humans. But if Cassie wasn't found, Gideon would blame himself. He again thought of his little sister and imagined how frightened she would be all alone in this scary place. He had never met Cassie, but she was probably a lot like Lilly, apart from the color of her skin.

Gideon came to a small hummock of solid soil where a vicious greenbrier, also known as the "devil's walking stick," blocked his way. He started to circle away from the vine's sharp thorns, then stopped abruptly. "Look!" He pointed to a piece of blue fabric clinging to the wicked plant.

"That's hers!" Horatio exclaimed, carefully removing the cloth. "She did come this way!"

Gideon hurried forward through the last of the undergrowth and stopped at the edge of the pond. Several tupelo gum trees grew out of the smelly water. Gideon glanced down and saw a few of the girl's bare footprints.

He pointed. "They lead toward the ridges." He began hurrying in that direction as fast as the peat allowed.

He remembered that herds of wild horned cattle now made their home on the dry ridges. They were descendants of domestic stock that had escaped into the swamp in Colonial times. They stayed on the higher, dry ridges where their split hooves didn't sink into the bog.

One morning Gideon and his father had come across the torn carcass of a scarred black bull. Tracks showed that it had staggered out of the swamp and died at the edge of the Tugwells' land. Nearby lay a large black bear, proof that the two big beasts had fought to the death.

Gideon's other memory was from two years ago when he and his father had been hunting here. They had left the marsh for easier walking on the ridges. Suddenly, a herd of cows with calves had charged from a small gully. Gideon and his father had escaped by plunging back into the sucking muck where the heavy animals could not follow.

★ ★

Gideon tried not to think of what a bear or wild cattle could do to a defenseless little girl. He called over his shoulder, "Come on! Hurry! Hurry!"

★ ★ ★ ★ ★

Emily's repeated efforts to get a pass had finally brought her up the chain of command to Colonel Pemberton of the provost marshal's office. An enlisted man silently ushered her into a plain room with only a simple desk, two chairs, and a Confederate flag on the wall. Her escort motioned her to take the straight-backed chair in front of the desk. She sat stiffly on the seat's edge.

The colonel didn't look up but continued bending over some papers on his desk. He wore a sky-blue kepi on his head with an elaborate scroll on its flat top, indicating his high rank. The sleeves of his blue uniform also had the fancy braid of rank.

Emily waited uneasily, hearing the dull boom of cannon fire outside the city. How long could the outnumbered South stand against overwhelming opposing forces? If she didn't quickly get her pass, Richmond might be overrun and she would never get to Illinois.

"So," Pemberton said brusquely, straightening up and looking her in the eyes. "You want a pass to leave our lines, and apparently you won't take no for an answer."

Alarmed at his hard tone, Emily licked her lips and managed a smile. "Sir. I grew up in Illinois, and—"

He waved her to silence. "I've read your file, so I know about you. Your strong support of the Union and antislavery sentiments are documented here. If you are allowed to leave our lines, I have to be very careful that no Confederate military secrets go with you."

"I know nothing of such secrets!"

"Even if I'm satisfied that you're telling the truth, I still can't let you leave without a chaperon. I don't see yours listed—"

★ ★

"Chaperon?" she interrupted. "Nothing was ever said before about needing—"

"Well, you do!" Pemberton broke in harshly. "You're only thirteen. I can't issue a pass unless you have a proper chaperon with proven loyalty to the Confederacy."

Dismayed, Emily protested, "Sir, I have been trying for many months to get this pass. Not one of the officers has ever mentioned needing a chaperon."

"That's regrettable." He stood, towering over her. "When you get one, you may again apply here."

Emily's outspoken nature made her leap to her feet. "Sir, I have met all previous conditions this office has put upon me! Now I have a feeling that nothing I do is going to make any difference. With respect, sir, if I get a chaperon, will I be issued a pass?"

He glowered at her. "You're a saucy one, so let me say it plainly. You're under an ongoing investigation. If anything suspicious turns up about you, you'd better plan on spending the rest of the war here in the South!"

# HARD CHOICES
# IN THE SWAMP

As Sergeant Kretzschmar violently swung his pick handle toward Nat's head, the teen ducked. The club smashed solidly against his left shoulder blade. He cried out as pain shot through him, and the soldier drew his hand back for another blow.

Nat tried to leap aside, throwing up his left arm to protect his head. The second strike numbed his forearm. He rapidly backed away, clutching the arm with his bloody and blistered right hand.

"Sergeant! Stop!"

Out of the corner of his eye, Nat saw another soldier in blue uniform and kepi bearing down on the scene. Nat didn't take his eyes off his attacker even when the newcomer demanded, "Why're you hitting him?"

"Insubordination, Major Buckner. These black devils won't work unless—"

"You have no authority to strike him!" the officer interrupted sternly. "I warned you before. These blacks are contraband of war and are not to be mistreated. Get rid of that club!"

"Begging your pardon, sir, but—"

"Sergeant, you heard my order." Major Buckner's voice rose sharply. "Is that clear?"

"Yes, sir, but—"

"No 'buts,' Sergeant! Rather, Private! I'm tired of talking to

★ ★

you. You're reduced in rank for repeatedly failing to obey a superior officer's orders." The major glared at the noncommissioned officer, then turned to Nat. "How badly are you hurt?" he asked quietly.

"I don't know, Master . . . uh . . . sir." Nat replied with a shrug that made him wince with pain.

"Where did you learn to speak proper English?"

Nat was startled. In the excitement, he had forgotten to use the common slave dialect. "My first master taught me, Mas . . . sir."

"Do you also read?"

"Yes, sir."

"I see. What's your name?"

"I am called Nat."

"Very well, Nat. Report immediately to the field hospital and tell the surgeon that Major Buckner said to have you checked out. When you're through, ask directions to my tent and report to me there. Is that clear?"

"Yes, sir." Nat watched the officer stride away, then turned toward the sergeant, whose face was flushed dark red with anger.

He thrust it close to Nat's and growled, "You got me busted, black boy! You're going to pay for that!"

★ ★ ★ ★ ★

Beyond the shallow pond with the tupelo gum trees, the unsteady peat gave way to more solid footing at the base of a series of long, low ridges that rose above the bog. Gideon vainly looked for more little footprints, but he was confident that the lost girl had gone that way because the traveling was easier.

"There are bears and wild cattle on these ridges," the boy told Fletcher and Horatio as they caught up with him. "I doubt bears would bother anyone unless they're cornered, but those herds of cattle are mean. I've been chased by them."

Heading for the nearest ridge, Gideon briefly described his

experiences. He shifted the heavy muzzle loader to the ready position as they left the dark, gloomy marsh with its dank smell of stagnant water and dense canopy of trees.

There were still no tracks, but Gideon expressed hope that they might see Cassie when they reached the top of the ridge. In one of the swamp's few open areas where he could see the sky, Gideon noticed high clouds had formed. They warned of possible rain and a coming night that would be darker than usual. The late afternoon sun slanted, making long shadows, the first Gideon had seen since entering the swamp.

At the ridge top, he stopped, breathing hard, to quickly glance in all directions. Fletcher and Horatio did the same, but nothing alive was visible. A couple hundred yards ahead, a small stand of trees rose like silent sentinels above the ridge. The strange stillness lingered, broken only by the distant baying of the two hounds.

Gideon's hopes began to fade, but he tried to speak with confidence. "If we call out for her, we might attract any wild cattle hiding in those trees or gullies. But if we don't—"

"Let's call," Horatio interrupted.

All three shouted, then vainly listened.

Suddenly, Horatio stiffened. "Listen! Hear that?"

Gideon cocked his head and held his breath. He shook his head and glanced at Fletcher, who shrugged.

Horatio insisted, "I heard something in the trees." He began running toward them, calling Cassie's name.

Gideon and Fletcher ran after him. Gideon fretted about the inadequate musket. It could fire only once before having to be reloaded—a process that would take Gideon about four minutes. If they stumbled upon a lone aggressive bull and Gideon didn't bring him down with the first shot, there would be no time to reload. Gideon and the men could climb trees if necessary, but that would cost them valuable time in finding the girl. Safety would then depend on outrunning the animal into the bog, where it could not follow. If there was a herd . . .

Gideon refused to finish his thought.

Horatio reached the trees a few steps ahead of Gideon and Fletcher. They cautiously entered the deep shadows, where bushes resembled motionless cattle.

A low, rumbling snort instantly made the short hairs on the back of Gideon's head stand on end and goose bumps erupt on his arms. He lifted the weapon, trying to remain calm so his one shot would be true. He whispered, "That sounds like an angry bull."

"It is!" Fletcher whispered, then pointed. "See him? Get down!"

Gideon and Horatio followed Fletcher's example of dropping to the ground so they couldn't be easily detected.

A couple hundred yards ahead, a large black bull with immense horns trotted awkwardly out of a gully and onto the top of the ridge. He stopped, raised his head, and bawled loudly. A herd of small, skinny black cows with wicked-looking horns followed him. Three half-grown calves trotted close behind the herd.

Gideon whispered, "They must have caught our smell, but they can't locate us."

The bull bellowed again, lowered his head, and pawed dirt with his forepaws before Gideon added, "Hear that? Sounds as if he has an echo."

"No," Fletcher said softly, "that's another bull farther down the ridge. Maybe this first one didn't really smell us, but he's challenging the other one."

Gideon whispered, "What do you think? Shall we go back into the swamp and then try to get past them?"

Horatio exclaimed softly under his breath, "Look!" He quickly pushed some short grass aside and held up another small torn piece of blue cloth. "That's hers! She went this way!"

Gideon felt proud of his decision to climb the ridge; there was still hope. But now they had to deal with not only threatening rain, night coming on fast, and a lost little girl, but also

★ ★

fighting bulls and a herd of wild cattle.

The boy didn't say anything, knowing that the men understood their situation. If they turned back now, they could return to safety before the rain started. Once it started, however, they would no longer be able to see landmarks and would be easy prey for poisonous snakes or treacherous bog areas. But if Cassie was still alive, her chances of surviving the night were slim.

Horatio said, "You two go back if you want, but I'm going on. Could I have the gun?"

"There's no need. I'll go with you," Gideon said, then he glanced at Fletcher, who nodded approval.

Gideon stuck his forefinger in his mouth to moisten it, then held it up. "Wind's from there." He pointed. "The cattle can't smell us if we go downwind. Keep low and hope that bull is so busy threatening the other one that they don't see us. Maybe we can circle around them."

Horatio warned, "Keep alert in case Cassie is between those two bulls."

Suddenly, a shrill scream came from ahead of the bellowing black bull on the ridge.

"That's her!" Horatio yelled, the cattle forgotten. "Cassie! I'm coming!" He broke into a wild run.

"Wait!" Gideon cried as the screaming continued. "Wait for the gun!"

The frantic father didn't reply. He raced on toward the terrorized shrieks, which were suddenly mixed with the bellowing of the two bulls.

Gideon and Fletcher threw caution to the wind and ran, flat out, toward the sounds.

*I've only got one shot, even if we do get there in time!* Gideon thought.

★　★　★　★　★

For hours, Emily had gone from one wounded soldier to

★ ★

another, ministering in a small hospital building while she suffered mental anguish over the colonel's unexpected demand that she find a chaperon. She had explained the situation to Mrs. Stonum, who sympathized but couldn't offer any help.

With a great effort of will, she shoved her own needs aside to concentrate on the wounded men. She brushed away swarms of flies, read the Bible aloud, or encouraged the men, depending on what each seemed to want. One requested a song. She protested that she didn't have much of a singing voice, but he insisted, and the other men joined in the request.

She softly raised her voice in "Amazing Grace," and the suffering men controlled their moaning to listen. She saw tears on their pain-wracked faces as she finished the final refrain. She heard faint sniffling, but otherwise there was an emotional silence.

Emily had tears in her eyes when Mrs. Stonum entered the outside door and motioned for Emily to leave. She whispered a final word of hope to the men, then stepped outside into the late afternoon sun.

The widow looked haggard. "One of the ambulance drivers in the main hospital kindly offered to drive us home. Are you ready?"

Emily nodded and sighed heavily. "It breaks my heart to see such fine young men with such terrible wounds. Yet they never complain. Even in their agony, they're always so polite."

Mrs. Stonum started walking through the open spaces between the other buildings toward the main hospital wing with Emily beside her. "Yes, I've been struck by that same wonderful spirit, regardless of which color uniform they wear."

"I've gotten so I don't pay much attention to which side they're on," Emily replied. "Their blood is all the same color."

"I'm so sick of this war!" the widow exclaimed. "I'm worn out emotionally from seeing all those poor wounded boys and knowing that more are coming. And I'm so tired that even my bones ache. Yet that's nothing compared to what those soldiers are going through."

"I'm tired, too," Emily admitted, "yet somehow I've never felt so useful, either."

"You still want to go back to Illinois?"

"Oh yes. That's my home." Emily saw an opening to mention an idea she had about a chaperon. "I've thought of everyone I know who might go with me, but there's only one person I'd like—you."

"Me? That's very flattering, but there's no way I can go off and leave all these wounded boys."

"What will you do if Richmond falls?"

"There will still be wounded; undoubtedly many more than now as the fighting intensifies. I'll stay and do what I can."

"I've heard some of the soldiers talking among themselves. They say the Confederates will burn the city if they can't stop General McClellan's army. What if your house is destroyed?"

"I don't know. It's all I've got left, but even if it burns, I still will have lost less than those who were wounded or gave their lives."

Emily remembered the anguish she had suffered when she had had to leave the home where she had grown up. Her family was dead, and the house still stood, but it hurt to think of never being able to live there again.

She forced the thought away to say, "Thousands of people are fleeing this city every day, just as thousands more are arriving. You don't have to stay." Emily didn't want to sound desperate, but she felt close to it.

She continued. "Nobody would blame you if you left. You're well known for all the help you give the doctors, and your patriotism can't be questioned. Why, you could easily get a pass through Confederate lines. Besides, you've worked so hard you deserve some rest. My friends in Illinois would welcome you if you went with me."

Mrs. Stonum shook her head. "There can be no rest for anyone until this cruel war is over, my dear. Have you considered all the ladies you've met at church? One of them might go with you."

"There's no one, and I've thought of everyone. I wish you would go with me."

"I sympathize with you, Emily, especially your concern about getting across the lines in case this city is captured. But I can't leave my post in this crisis."

"Won't you please at least think about it?"

"I'm sorry, Emily, but as long as I have my health and can be useful to these poor boys, I must stay and do what I can."

Emily was deeply disappointed. "I understand," she said sadly, "but I had to ask."

★ ★ ★ ★ ★

There had been no further screams from the little girl, making Gideon fearful that something terrible had happened to her. But she was still out of sight beyond a small rise from where the angry bellowing of the two bulls could be heard.

Both men outran Gideon, so they reached the top of the rise ahead of him. They stopped and motioned for him to hurry up with the gun. The big black bull with immense horns had stopped in front of a snag of tree, which had broken off at the point of the two lower limbs.

The top had fallen so that one end rested on the ground and the other was caught in the tree crotch, about six feet off the ground. The little girl crouched there, her back to Gideon and the men. She had wrapped both arms around her legs, which were drawn up almost to her chin.

A second bull, slightly smaller and a somewhat lighter shade of black than the first one, stood on the far side of the girl's precarious perch. His horns viciously hooked the air just below Cassie's feet.

At the approach of the challenger, the bull that had chased the girl up the tree turned from her and bellowed loudly. He

★ ★

tossed his massive head and began pawing up clumps of earth with his forefeet. The bigger animal stopped and also started throwing up dirt. The cows and half-grown calves halted a safe distance away and watched the bulls.

Gideon whispered to Fletcher, "What'll we do? I can take one out with my single shot, but—"

"Save it!" he interrupted. "Cassie's safe enough for the moment. We have to wait for an opening."

Horatio shook his head. "If they fight and bump into that tree, she'll get knocked down."

"I know!" Fletcher broke in. "If that happens, I'll run in and distract the bulls. One of you grab the girl—"

"She's my daughter!" Horatio broke in. "I'll go get her and run for the swamp."

With a final bellow, the first bull charged past the tree toward his opponent. They met with heads down and horns clicking, staggering, pushing, and making deep rumbling sounds in their big chests.

Gideon sucked in his breath when the two combatants brushed against the dead tree. Cassie screamed as it swayed dangerously. She swiveled around to regain her seat, the whites of her eyes showing total terror.

Then she looked away from the animals and shrieked, "Papa! I'm scared! Come get me, Papa!"

He reached for the gun. "Let me have that!"

"Wait!" Gideon exclaimed, twisting away so that Horatio's hand just brushed the muzzle loader. "Getting one will let the other bull come after us! Look! See what's happening?"

He pointed with his free hand toward the bulls. The smaller one suddenly broke off the fight. He turned and ran awkwardly down the ridge away from the people. Bellowing in triumph, the victor lumbered after him. The cows and calves stood with heads up, watching the humans.

"Now, Horatio!" Fletcher shouted. "Go! Go!"

The little girl's father was already moving, rushing wildly

★ ★

toward his daughter, calling reassuringly to her. Fletcher raced after him.

Gideon didn't dare watch them any longer. One quick look showed him that the bulls were still running away, so he shifted his gaze to the nearby cows. They took a few tentative steps toward him, snorting noisily, threatening to charge.

Gideon's heart was pounding, and he knew he couldn't afford to miss if he had to shoot. He dropped to one knee to give himself better support and quickly brought the heavy weapon to his shoulder.

A large cow started toward him, shaking her head. He held his breath and took careful aim between her eyes. If she was the leader, he might stop the whole herd by taking her out. But if they all charged, he would have an empty gun and no time to reload. He wondered if he could outrun the herd to the relative safety of the swamp.

Fletcher exclaimed from behind him, "We've got Cassie! Come on, Gideon! Get out of here before they attack us!"

Leaping up, Gideon yelled and threw both hands up in the air, hoping to scare the animals. Snorting, all turned as one and ran away—except for the large cow that appeared to be the leader. She lowered her head and charged.

Gideon's heart suddenly seemed to burst, but he resisted the temptation to run. There was no time to re-aim, so he quickly pointed the gun at the animal and fired.

# DANGER ON ALL SIDES

Emily ignored her weariness from working at the hospital, while she fixed dinner at Mrs. Stonum's home. Hannah had not returned from the munitions factory when Emily and the widow sat down to eat.

Mrs. Stonum bowed her head and said a brief blessing before looking toward the parlor. "I wonder what's keeping Hannah? I don't like my girls being out after dark. Richmond is so full of crime now."

"I'm sure she'll be along shortly," Emily replied, regretting the unresolved tension between her roommate and herself.

The widow looked thoughtfully across the table at Emily. "You look a little tense. Are you all right?"

"Just a little tired, as I'm sure you are. I'm also feeling somewhat embarrassed about being so insistent about you becoming my chaperon."

"There's no need to be embarrassed, Emily. I understand how anxious you are to get home to Illinois. You'll find someone else."

The front door opened and Hannah called, "I'm home."

"I'm glad," Mrs. Stonum called. "Please join us. Emily kept your plate warm."

"Thanks," Hannah replied. "I'm very hungry."

Emily hurried to the kitchen and uncovered the plate she had placed on the back of the wood-burning stove. She reentered the dining room as Hannah sat down.

"Emily and I were concerned about your being out so late," Mrs. Stonum said. "Did something happen at work?"

Hannah met Emily's eyes as she set the plate before her. "Sort of. I was just about to leave for the day when two men from the provost marshal's office arrived."

Startled, Emily blurted, "Provost marshal?"

"Yes." There was a hint of smugness in Hannah's tone, as though she enjoyed tormenting Emily by not immediately explaining why the officials had been there.

Mrs. Stonum asked the question foremost in Emily's mind. "What did they want?"

"Nothing much. They just said they had to talk to me. So I stayed, then they drove me home."

Emily was now sure that Hannah was deliberately dragging the topic out without getting to the point. It was difficult for Emily to wait for details, but she forced herself to be quiet.

Mrs. Stonum asked, "What did they say?"

"One did all the talking. A colonel named Pember . . . something."

"Lyman Pemberton?" Emily asked, her alarm rising.

"Yes, that's it. He asked some questions about you." Hannah slowly unfolded her napkin before adding, "He knew we were roommates and wondered what you were like."

Emily licked her suddenly dry lips. "Oh?" She tried to make it sound noncommittal, but anxiety seized her. More than ever, she wished she had been able to ease the strain that had existed between them since she had refused to share her secret about Fitzhugh.

Mrs. Stonum said, "I'm sure you said helpful things about Emily because the man was obviously investigating her about the pass she wants."

"Of course." Hannah gave Emily a faint smile. "I didn't say anything bad about you."

"Thank you."

"The only thing that seemed to interest him," Hannah continued offhandedly, "was when I mentioned that Fitzhugh carries your letters for nothing."

Emily felt as if an icy hand had suddenly grabbed her heart. Hannah was obviously enjoying a little game of mental torture. Emily forced herself to remain calm.

The widow asked impatiently, "What did the colonel say about that?"

Hannah took a bite and chewed slowly before answering. "Nothing. He just thanked me, then drove me here."

"That sounds logical," Mrs. Stonum cheerfully told Emily. "He's probably trying to expedite your pass."

"That's what I figured," Hannah admitted. "But he said something about Richmond being full of spies, and how we all had to be careful."

Emily stared at Hannah, who continued eating. She seemed to be well pleased with herself, as if she was punishing Emily for keeping Fitzhugh's secret. Emily had not done anything wrong, yet she sensed trouble. What if Fitzhugh had not told her the truth about her letters?

★ ★ ★ ★ ★

On Saturday, Gideon, his family, and Fletcher drove the wagon into the village to check for mail and to buy a few necessities they could not grow or make for themselves. It seemed almost everyone they met had read the *Villager*'s lengthy account of how the little girl had been rescued from the swamp.

Mrs. Yates, who had written the story, quoted the grateful father at length. Gideon was flustered yet pleased to be credited with using common sense and woodsmanship to find the girl after his hounds failed to follow her trail. The news item also mentioned that when Gideon looked back after firing the gun and escaping into the swamp, the wild cow that had charged him was seen running away, apparently unharmed.

★ ★

Mr. Zeldman, the balding little owner of the local mercantile store, gave Gideon and each of his siblings a piece of hard candy as a reward. There never had been money for such treats. The children enjoyed their sweets while Zeldman finished filling the Tugwells' five-gallon coal-oil can from a fifty-gallon drum. He stuck a potato on the spout as a stopper.

"Mrs. Tugwell," he said in a voice loud enough for the other shoppers to hear, "you are blessed to have such a fine, brave son."

Gideon dropped his head to stare unseeingly at the wooden floor with its smell of oily sawdust.

"I am proud of all my children," she replied, wistfully touching a bolt of cheerful calico cloth.

A male voice asked from the front door, "Even if they go against their own kind?"

Gideon hadn't heard William Lodge enter, and for a moment Gideon didn't grasp the hint of disapproval.

His mother understood at once, and she said crisply, "A lost little girl would have died if it hadn't been for my son and those two men. Any one of God's people is our kind of people, regardless of color."

William's lip curled disdainfully. "I'm not surprised to hear such a foolish remark from white trash."

Gideon didn't remember moving, but suddenly he was across the store, his face thrust close to William's. "You take that back!" he said through clenched teeth.

Startled, William took a couple of quick steps backward, knocking over a bushel of potatoes. They rolled across the floor, causing William to sprawl on top of them.

"Gideon!" His mother's voice sounded pleadingly from across the store, but it didn't really register on him. He reached down quickly and grabbed the front of William's fancy store-bought shirt.

Vaguely, Gideon remembered that William had always outweighed him by at least forty pounds. Gideon had also suffered

★ ★

many beatings over the years when he was a skinny, wiry kid. But now his sudden fury at the insult to his mother and the knowledge that he was almost as tall and heavy as his adversary made Gideon bold.

"You tell her you're sorry!" he ordered, yanking on the shirt so hard that it tore. "Do it now!"

For the first time in his life, Gideon saw fear in William's eyes. "Let me up, and step back," the boy pleaded.

Nodding, Gideon obeyed, watching William carefully get to his feet. Suddenly remembering the others, Gideon looked toward them, ashamed for having lost control of his temper.

In that instant, William spun on his heels and dashed out the open door. Too late, Gideon darted after him while his mother's voice pleaded for him to stop.

Contritely, Gideon obeyed, watching William sprint across the dusty street toward the fancy town coach with the ornate Briarstone Plantation crest on the door.

"Drive, you old fool!" William ordered the gray-haired black driver sitting on the high outside seat. William jerked the door open and plunged inside.

Gideon's temper cooled as the matched bay team pulled away so fast that the vehicle swayed dangerously.

William stuck his head out of the open door window to yell as he passed, "Now you've done it, Gideon Tugwell! Nothing can save you from what's going to happen!"

★ ★ ★ ★ ★

Nat finished polishing Major Buckner's boots and placed them beside the bunk in his military tent. "All done," he said. "What do you want me to do now?"

The officer looked up from a pan of water, where he had been washing. "You sure you don't mind doing all these menial chores, Nat?"

The runaway teenage slave had long ago learned to smile and hide his feelings toward white folks. "I don't mind because

★ ★

I'm free here to come and go. That's better than anything I've ever had in my life."

"If rumors coming out of Washington are true, President Lincoln is soon going to issue an emancipation proclamation that will free you slaves."

"Can't be too soon to suit me," Nat replied, trying to sound cheerful, although he secretly doubted the truth of the rumor.

The major said, "I can appreciate how you must feel. I hear that the president is just waiting for a major military victory to make the announcement. The way we're moving on Richmond, he may soon have that triumph. Then you and all slaves in rebellious states will be free."

Nat grinned. In the few days he had been assigned to the major, Nat had sensed that he could be more candid with him than any other white man he'd ever met. "Seems to me it's taking more than talk to make the Confederates do what Mr. Lincoln says."

"It's just a matter of time, Nat." The major dried his face, saying through the cloth, "There's no way the South can hold out against the North. Everything is on our side: factories, manpower, munitions, food, trains, and all the other necessary elements. The South is short of everything and getting shorter."

It pleased Nat that he was allowed to engage in a conversation without being reminded that he was a slave, an inferior being, as he had been told all his life. Even though he was still doing a slave's work, he had one very great privilege. At night, he had a pass to visit any nearby Union camp, where he could search for his mother and sister. The only stipulation was that he be back at the major's tent before reveille, the morning bugle.

"Nat," the officer said, his tone indicating a change in subjects, "I've passed the word along to my fellow officers in each camp where I've been. If your mother and sister are working

★ ★

in any of their laundries, I'll hear about it. Then the three of you can be reunited."

Nat was touched. No white man had ever treated him with such kindness. "Thank you, sir," he said sincerely.

"Suppose you do find them. What then?"

Instantly, Nat became wary. He had no intention of telling about his contact with the secret Underground Railroad in Richmond. Of course, if the capital fell, there was no telling if Edward Reverdy would remain as a conductor.

Maybe Reverdy had already fled the capital, as thousands had done. If so, Nat didn't know of anyone else who could start his mother and sister on the way to freedom in the North or Canada.

Nat answered carefully. "I'm hopeful they'll be able to escape to freedom in the North, sir. But right now, I am just concentrating on trying to find them."

"I hope you do. Tell me something: Where did you learn to be so self-assured?"

"My mother taught me before we were sold apart . . . " Nat hesitated, not sure he should trust any white man with his mother's philosophy. But Nat decided to tell Major Buckner. "Sir, she used to say, 'Winning is in the mind and not the muscles.' I try to remember that."

"She sounds like a remarkable woman. I hope you find her before we move on toward Richmond again."

"Move?" Nat was startled, sensing his search might be forcibly ended. "When?"

"Any time now. The rumor is that General McClellan smells victory and is eager to claim it. I guess he's going to throw his entire army into a major push to seize Richmond. Naturally, I want you to come with me."

Nat understood that was a compliment, but it went against his own plans. It would be much harder searching for his family if all the Union camps were on the move.

"Yes, sir. Thank you, sir," he said with a forced smile. But behind that cheerful expression he had a sickening feeling in his heart.

★　★　★　★　★

After Fletcher finished supper with the Tugwells, he asked to be excused, but Gideon's mother stopped him.

"You seem worried," she said. "Is it because of William's threat in the store?"

He glanced around the table at the children, then across the lamp to their mother. "I don't like to express my opinion in a family matter, Mrs. Tugwell."

"We value your opinion," she assured him. "Let's sit on the porch while you tell us what you think." She stood, leaving food on her plate. "Gideon, would you join us? This involves you. The rest of you, finish your supper, then, Ben, help your sisters with the dishes."

They sent up a howl of protest, but she silenced them with a glance, then proceeded through the front door, which Fletcher held open for her. Gideon followed them both into the soft darkness. They sat side by side on the top step and silently studied the stars for a moment.

"Mr. Fletcher," Gideon's mother began, her voice low, "what were you thinking about in there?"

He took a deep breath and let it out before replying. "You have a good crop of oats and early wheat. I want to help Gideon get it to market. It should bring enough cash money to pay your taxes and defeat William Lodge's plan to take over this property."

Mrs. Tugwell said softly, "You are very kind."

Gideon declared, "William can't stop us now!"

"Don't underestimate him," Mrs. Tugwell cautioned. "Besides, getting to market won't be easy. The Yankees control Manassas Junction, where you and your father sold our wheat last year. The only other market is Richmond, and the Yankees might burn that before you get there."

She added firmly, "But the crop is useless in the field; it must go to market. If it's lost on the way, at least we've tried. But if we do nothing, we'll lose this place to taxes for sure. None of us wants that to happen."

Gideon was surprised at his mother's firm tone. She had always allowed her husband to make major decisions.

She continued. "William may try to stop us if he knows you're going. He must not find out until it's too late."

Gideon reached out and gently touched his mother's hands. "I guess Mr. Fletcher and I could load the wagon in the barn, where people passing along the road wouldn't see us. Then if we could start out before dawn—"

"Excuse me," Fletcher interrupted, "that could work, but I have another concern. What will William do when he finds out that we have already left with the crop?"

Gideon declared stoutly, "Once we're on the road, he can't stop us."

Fletcher mused, "I meant, what if he attacks this place while we're gone?"

"He wouldn't dare!" Gideon cried. "Nobody would bother a widow and small children except Yankees!"

"William might," Mrs. Tugwell observed softly. "Oh, he wouldn't do it himself, but he could hire someone."

"Like Barley Cobb!" Gideon exclaimed. "But what would he do? Try to scare you to death while Mr. Fletcher and I are gone?"

Mrs. Tugwell didn't answer, but after a moment, Fletcher cleared his throat. "We'll have a wagonload of wheat and no room for the oats. They have to wait until we get back." He paused before adding ominously, "Oats ready to harvest will burn very quickly."

"What?" Gideon cried.

"Mr. Fletcher is right," his mother said. "Fire could not only destroy our crop but even this house. Besides, if William gets this place he will surely tear it down or burn it anyway.

★ ★

No matter what we do, there is great risk."

No one spoke for a long moment as they all considered the terrible truth of that statement.

"Mr. Fletcher," Gideon's mother finally said, "What would you suggest?"

"I've thought about it a lot." His voice was barely audible in the darkness. "Horatio told me after his little girl was rescued that he and his freedman friends would help us in any way they could. Maybe he would keep an eye on this place while Gideon and I go to market."

Gideon leaped to his feet. "That's a good idea!"

"I'm not so sure," his mother replied. "You know how William feels about black people, slave or free. We can't ask Horatio and his friends to take risks for us."

Gideon moaned. "Then what will we do?"

Nobody answered, but Gideon knew they had to decide between two difficult choices. If they made the wrong one, everything they had in the world would be lost.

★ ★

# ARRESTED!

Emily slept fitfully the last night of May. She dreamed that Colonel Pemberton, the provost marshal, extended a pass so she could leave Richmond for Illinois. As she reached for it, he snatched it back because she had not yet found a chaperon.

"Emily, wake up!" Mrs. Stonum's voice was brusque, making the girl's eyes pop open. "Hurry, Emily!" the widow urged, "there's a terrible battle going on at Seven Pines, seven miles east of here. We're needed at the hospital. A driver is waiting downstairs."

Dawn was just breaking outside the second-story bedchamber Emily shared with Hannah. Her roommate's empty bed showed that she had already left for her twelve-hour shift at the munitions factory.

Mrs. Stonum urged, "Dress quickly. I've heard the ambulances rumbling through the streets for hours, but I just now got word of how fierce the fighting has been."

The urgency in the widow's tone was so strong that Emily moved in alarm. She dressed quickly, grabbed her bonnet, and, without eating breakfast, hurried with Mrs. Stonum to the waiting buggy.

The elderly white driver warned, "Prepare yourselves, ladies. Casualities are the worst I've seen, and the battle is still going on at Seven Pines."

Emily thought she had seen enough of horrible wounds,

but it was nothing compared to what she saw when the rig neared the capitol area. Long lines of ox carts, farm wagons, and ambulances flowed from the battlefield into the city streets. Every vehicle bore horribly wounded men toward medical help that could still be many hours away.

The driver explained, "The hospitals and tents can't hold all the wounded. They're being taken to warehouses, churches, hotels, and private homes. Around this next corner, you'll see that some are just being unloaded on the sidewalks. Every available woman, rich and poor, young and old, is trying to help. I even heard that the shortage is so great that for the first time, girls will help nurse."

As the buggy turned the corner, Emily gasped at the fearsome sight. Union and Confederate soldiers lay side by side. Some had a haversack under their heads; a few had an army blanket. But most men had nothing under or over them. Emily's horrified eyes misted at the sight of the mutilated bodies, heads, arms, and legs. She involuntarily turned away and fought to keep from being sick.

After turning east on Broad Street and arriving at the Chimborazo Hospital, Emily recognized the doctor who had once rudely ordered her away from helping the wounded because she was too young.

"Mrs. Stonum," he said gruffly, "you know what to do." He turned to Emily. "You, young lady, report to the surgeon in that first building over there. Do whatever he tells you."

She nodded and entered the building, making her way through the moaning wounded toward a haggard surgeon in a bloody apron with a saw in his hand. He didn't even look up but ordered, "Start at the first man and do what you can for him."

She glanced at the row of men and flinched at the horrible sound of the surgeon's saw on a leg bone. At the first man in line, she knelt, barely noticing his grimy blue uniform. She took one quick glance at his bloody left arm and the pain-filled

★ ★

eyes staring dully out of a face blackened with gunpowder.

He whispered, "Water, please. I'm so thirsty."

"I'll get some and be right back." She stood and glanced around uncertainly, looking for a water bucket.

"Emily? Is that you?"

Startled, she recognized the voice. She whirled and again looked down at the wounded soldier. "Brice!" she cried. "Brice Barlow!"

★ ★ ★ ★ ★

Gideon had just finished writing in his journal when his mother entered the barn. She motioned for him to come down from the haymow. When he stood before her by the manger, she asked, "What were you writing about?"

"I was trying to set down my thoughts about God making all men of one blood. It's hard to accept."

"We're all God's children; you know that."

"Yes, but a slave, Mama! The Supreme Court ruled that Negroes are property, not people. The Bible is full of stories about slavery, but I don't see where God ever condemned it."

"When you rescued Horatio's little girl from the swamp, did you doubt for one minute that her father's heart wasn't as broken as a white man's would be at the thought of losing his child?"

"He was scared and hurting like any person would be, Mama. But all my life I've heard that slaves are inferior to us white people. I can't tell you how many preachers I've heard say that slavery is God's plan for blacks."

"I wish I could say something wise to help you, but all I can do is pray that the Lord will guide you until you reach your own decision. Right now I need to talk to you of getting our wheat to market."

He fell into step beside her as she walked out of the barn. "I thought it was already decided that Mr. Fletcher and I would take it to Richmond."

★ ★

"Yes, we're agreed on that, but Mr. Fletcher just told me that he feels we're going to have an abundant crop. In fact, he just said he thinks that with inflation and shortages, we could not only make enough to pay the taxes but also have enough to live on for a year."

"Really? Wouldn't that be wonderful?"

"It would be a real blessing. But remember that if the crop is seized by foraging troops—ours or Yankees—we can't pay the taxes. Then we'd lose this place."

Gideon stopped abruptly. "And you'd have to marry Barley Cobb! Is that what you mean?"

She didn't answer but lowered her eyes. Gideon's blood coursed hotly through his veins. "No, Mama! Don't even think about it!"

She raised her eyes and declared firmly, "I will not let my children go hungry, no matter what it costs me!"

Desperately, Gideon grasped at the first thought to pop into his head. "How about Mr. Fletcher? He's a good man! I like him, too!"

"You mustn't forget that we've only known him about two months. Besides, a woman has to be asked. Also, he's told us that when all our crops are in this fall, he's returning to the Shenandoah Valley."

"I don't want him to go, Mama!"

"It's his decision, not yours or mine. I'm sure you've heard the news that General Jackson—the one they're now calling 'Stonewall'—has defeated the Union armies in the valley. He's become a legend because with a very small number of soldiers, he has cleared the Yankees out of all except a small part of that valley. It's too bad he can't be free to help defeat the invaders at Richmond. They're reported within five miles of there."

Gideon looked hard at his mother. "You mean, by the time we get there with our wheat, Richmond may be in Yankee hands?"

"General Joseph Johnston is defending the city as best he

★ ★

can. But since there is no place else to sell our crop, I pray that the city will still be in Confederate hands when you and Mr. Fletcher get there."

Gideon sighed. He wondered if there would be time to see Emily during their visit to the capital.

"We have one hope," Mrs. Tugwell said. "Mr. Fletcher says that the wheat will be ready about three weeks earlier than last year. So if Richmond still stands by the end of June . . . oh, look! Here comes Barley Cobb!"

Gideon gritted his teeth at the sight of the slave catcher riding his mule up the long lane from the public road. Gideon had not expected to see Cobb again after his mother twice ordered him off the place. *I wonder what he wants*, Gideon thought, and quickly added to himself, *Whatever it is, it's not going to be good*.

★ ★ ★ ★ ★

Emily was so excited about seeing Brice Barlow that she wanted to stay with him. However, there were so many other wounded that she was forced to move on down the rows of suffering soldiers. She worked automatically, holding cups of water to pale lips, washing gunpowder from pain-wracked faces, and helping sufferers to a more comfortable position.

She spoke soft words of hope and encouragement, prayed for those who asked, and tried to keep from weeping at the look of gratitude on tortured faces. But when some older, more experienced women took over, she made her way back to Brice. She told him not to talk while she did what little she could to comfort him. But he wanted to tell her what happened, so she listened.

"My horse was shot from under me." Brice's words came haltingly, broken by the spasms of pain that made him grimace. But slowly he continued. "I leaped clear of the saddle and crouched behind his body as a shield. My carbine was under him, so I picked up a rifle from a dead infantryman.

"My face got all black from tearing the cartridges open with my teeth to load the gun after each shot. I didn't see the Rebel that slipped up and shot me."

He glanced at the bloody wound above his left elbow and was silent for several seconds.

"How . . . how bad am I hurt?" he finally asked in a low tone edged with fear. "Will it have to be cut off?"

Emily had been around the wounded long enough to know that many died after having an arm or leg amputated. She hadn't seen how bad the actual wound was, but she tried to sound confident. "I'm sure it'll be all right. There are some fine surgeons here."

"I hope you're right, Emily. While I've got the chance, I want to say thanks for your letters. I didn't get many, but those meant a lot to me."

"I'm glad," she said sincerely.

He managed a weak smile. "Remember once when I told you that I'm going to marry you when you grow up?"

She felt a warm flush on her cheeks but was able to hide her embarrassment when a soldier down the row of men suddenly shrieked in pain. "I have to go," Emily told Brice, and she hurried to the man even though there was very little she could do for him. But until the surgeons came to care for him, she could hold his hand and speak quiet words of comfort. She was comforted by Brice's compliment and prayed that soon she would receive her pass. When she reached Illinois, she could tell Brice's mother and sister about his wound. They would surely learn about it through the printed casualty lists, but there would be no details.

Emily tried not to think about what would happen to Brice after he recovered. But in her heart, she already knew: He would be held in Richmond's Libby Prison. Emily shuddered at the thought of him remaining there until the war ended.

★ ★ ★ ★ ★

★ ★

Gideon marveled at Barley Cobb's nerve as he dismounted from his mule. He greeted the boy and his mother as cordially as if she had not twice ordered him off the farm. Then he said, "I see yore early summer wheat is comin' on right smart."

Gideon flared, "What were you doing on our land?"

"I was on the river," the slave catcher replied, ignoring the boy's challenging tone. "Looks like yore harvest will come a mite early. Two, maybe three weeks."

"What's your point, Cobb?" Mrs. Tugwell demanded.

Gideon noticed that she hadn't called him "mister." That was a sure sign she was doing it deliberately to keep the visitor from feeling welcome.

"I come to offer ye muh mule to haul yore waggin to market, seein' as how ye only got Hercules. Ye'll need two stout mules to pull a load as heavy as this one."

"I thank you kindly," Mrs. Tugwell replied coolly, "but we'll not need your help."

Shrugging, Cobb answered, "Suit yerse'f, Martha." He glanced around. "That one-handed gent moved on?"

"Mr. Fletcher's whereabouts is no concern of yours," Mrs. Tugwell snapped.

Gideon frowned, aware that if Cobb had been down on the river, he must have seen Fletcher working in the fields. That meant Cobb knew Fletcher was still around.

Mrs. Tugwell told the slave catcher, "Now, if you've said what you came to say, then you must excuse Gideon and me. We have work to do."

"Ain't quite finished, Martha. Ye heard tell about the new Virginia partisan law recently passed? About the rangers?"

"I've heard something about it. They're also called guerrillas, irregulars, and local service. They will join our soldiers defending us against the Yankees but will operate less formally."

"Rangers already been operating in the Shenandoah," Cobb said. "Hit-and-run fighting, mostly. Giving them blue-belly Yankees cat fits attacking and burning, then skippin' out o' sight. Me? Well," he sucked in his breath and threw out his chest proudly, "I'm a-gonna j'ine up an' fight them bluecoats around here."

"I haven't heard about any of them in this area," Mrs. Tugwell said tartly.

"Ain't jist Yankees in uniform I'm after, Martha. I aim to help hang their spies, who *ain't* in uniform."

Gideon didn't understand at first, but his mother did. "Mr. Fletcher is not a spy, and you know it! He lost his hand fighting for the Confederacy! Don't you dare say anything like that again, Cobb! Now, good day to you!"

The slave catcher sadly shook his head. "Martha, ye done tried my patience agin! How long do ye reckon I'll put up with—?"

"Good-bye!" Gideon's mother interrupted and angrily stalked away toward the house.

Gideon grinned appreciatively after her, then turned in time to see a look on Cobb's face that made the boy feel afraid.

★　★　★　★　★

As he had many nights before, Nat took his pass and made his way to the laundry area of nearby Union camps. It was discouraging because the camps were constantly moved during the Peninsular Campaign—even now, as the crucial Battle of Seven Pines raged on the outskirts of Richmond. Still, the young fugitive kept hoping.

He found three matronly black contraband women sitting outside their makeshift laundry rooms, smoking their pipes and talking among themselves. In the pale light of the nearby Union campfires and the reflected glow of a lamp inside the building, he skimmed the faces. All were strangers.

He asked the same question he had often posed. "Have you heard of a woman named Lucy who has a little girl called Cordelia?"

Before the women could answer, someone shrieked from

inside the laundry room. Nat joined the three women in turning toward the sound. A slender woman in her early thirties suddenly appeared in the doorway.

For a moment they both stared at each other, and Nat's heart leaped like a colt in springtime. "Mama?" he cried in a hoarse whisper.

"Nat! Oh, Nat!" She rushed out of the doorway, calling over her shoulder, "Cordelia! Your brother's come!"

Nat threw his arms around his mother and held her tight. "Oh, Mama! Mama!" he whispered brokenly. "I looked so long for you!"

"I knew you'd come, Nat." She was crying and laughing at the same time. "I knew it! I knew it!"

A little girl in pigtails ran up and shyly hid behind her mother's long skirt. Nat freed one hand and gently reached around to pull her toward him. "You've grown, little sister!" he exclaimed, aware that tears were flowing freely down his cheeks.

Nat's mother put her arms around both children. "Let's go someplace and talk," she urged. "We don't have much time because tomorrow this camp is moving and we don't know where."

"I know where you're going, Mama," Nat declared, his voice abruptly firming. He added in a whisper, "I'm going to get you to freedom on the Underground Railroad."

"Now, how you going to do that?"

"I don't know, Mama, but now that I've found you two, I'll find a way."

She smiled at him through her tears, which glistened in the firelight. "I see you remember what I told you."

"Yes, Mama. I never forgot that 'winning is in the mind and not the muscles.' Come on; let's talk fast."

★　★　★　★　★

It was late when Emily was driven to Mrs. Stonum's house,

★ ★

136

while the widow remained at the hospital. Emily had often been tired, but never so much as she was tonight. Still, she felt good inside. She had not only miraculously found Brice, but the same doctor who had recently rudely ordered her away from patients had this afternoon praised her for her volunteer work.

Emily started to remove her bonnet while mounting the steps to Mrs. Stonum's front porch. Emily planned to write Gideon about Brice. She would have the letter ready when Oliver Fitzhugh came around again.

Suddenly, she stopped, startled by two men who emerged from the shadows and approached her. She stepped back in alarm, but a male voice stopped her.

"Emily Lodge, remember me? Colonel Pemberton!"

"Oh!" she exclaimed, greatly relieved. "Have you come to give me the pass I need to get back to Illinois?"

"I'm afraid not. You're under arrest on charges of spying against the Confederacy!"

# ATTACK IN THE NIGHT

Major Buckner was writing a letter when Nat returned and hastily reported the exhilarating news that he had found his mother and sister. The officer congratulated him.

Nat shifted uncomfortably and looked at the floor of the major's tent. "There's just one problem, sir. I would like permission to go to Richmond right away."

Buckner studied Nat thoughtfully for a few seconds before answering. "I anticipated that if you found them, you might just run off without letting me know. I am proud of you for coming to ask permission."

Nat raised his eyes in gratitude. "You know why I must go, don't you, sir?"

"I'd guess that you want to make arrangements for your mother and sister to go north to freedom."

Nat admitted, "I have a contact in Richmond who can help—if he's still there."

"Does this have anything to do with the mysterious Underground Railroad I've heard about?"

"I beg your pardon, but I'd rather not answer that."

Nodding, Buckner commented, "I respect you for being discreet, Nat. I'll give you a pass that may help you but which some higher-ranking officer might not honor. It would be wise of you to avoid them if possible."

"Thank you, sir." Nat was so overcome that he blurted,

"You're the first white man who's ever treated me so kindly."

"Lots of people are prejudiced against others, Nat. It seems that's the only way they can feel superior. But there are many of us who don't feel that way."

"I'll remember," Nat replied.

"Good! Now go find a contraband teamster named Lorenzo. I trust him, and so does the general. I know he's given orders for Lorenzo to start tomorrow and drive the general's baggage wagon to just outside of Richmond. With a pass from the general, nobody's going to stop Lorenzo. Your pass will indicate you're accompanying him, so I doubt anyone will bother you, either."

"I'm very grateful, sir."

"You strike me as being worthy of being helped. You will be on your own once you reach Confederate lines. The pickets obviously won't honor my pass, but I'm sure that you will manage to somehow get into the city."

Buckner extended his right hand. "Good luck. I hope you and your family reach freedom."

★ ★ ★ ★ ★

Emily was questioned by Colonel Pemberton and the enlisted man in a small bare room at the provost marshal's headquarters. She sat on an uncomfortable stool, but there were no chairs or other furniture in sight. The men stood over her while her head swam from the totally unexpected arrest. She stared at the short chain connected to the hand irons on her wrists.

Pemberton towered above her in his dark blue jacket and pale blue cotton trousers. "All right, Emily," he said gruffly, "let's start over again. This time answer my questions so it will go easier on you."

"But I told you!" she flared, turning weary eyes imploringly up at him. "I am not a spy! I'm just trying to get home to Illinois—that's all." She had wept quietly on the ride downtown, but realizing that would do no good, she had determined to fight this unjust charge.

The colonel demanded, "Do you deny that you've made remarks about slavery being wrong?"

"It is, so I've said it. But that doesn't make me a spy! I also support President Lincoln, but that's my right! I believe in trying to keep the Union together."

"Have you given military secrets to anyone?"

"No, of course not! For one thing, I don't know any of your secrets. Even if I did, I don't know anybody to tell about them, and I wouldn't do that anyway."

"Then why does Oliver Fitzhugh deliver your letters free of charge?"

Emily hesitated before replying, "I can't tell you that."

"Why not?"

"Because I promised!"

"You promised Fitzhugh to provide him with all kinds of military facts in exchange for carrying your letters, didn't you?"

Slowly, the truth dawned on Emily. Fitzhugh had asked her to give him "news" about the Federal troops she talked to. It had made sense to her that he would like to know such information to pass along to family and friends on his mail delivery route. But suddenly she sensed a possible other side to his agreement.

She asked, "What's he got to do with this?"

"We arrested him on charges of spying, and he named you as his accomplice."

Emily stared, feeling her mouth drop open. Her tongue suddenly went dry and almost seemed to click when she spoke again. "He didn't!"

"Yes, he did. He signed a confession and is being held pending his execution by hanging."

"Hang. . . ?" Emily cried, unable to finish saying the dreaded word aloud.

★ ★

"Yes. We hang spies instead of shooting them because that's what they deserve for aiding the enemy."

"You're probably going to try hanging me, too, and for something I didn't do!"

"There's only one way to avoid that, Emily. Tell me the entire truth right now, and I'll try to get you off with a lighter sentence."

"I'm only thirteen! You wouldn't hang me!"

"I wouldn't be proud of it, but what you and Fitzhugh did got many of our men killed. I'm going to step outside for a few minutes to give you time to think. Confession is the only way to save your life!"

"But I'm innocent! I didn't do anything—!"

"Five minutes, Emily," the colonel interrupted and walked out, followed by the enlisted man.

Helpless and alone, Emily sank onto the stool, her mind and heart about to burst in anguish.

★ ★ ★ ★ ★

After finding the contraband teamster named Lorenzo and explaining that Major Buckner had ordered Nat to accompany him, he returned to his mother and sister. They sat outside the large tent where the laundry workers slept and talked. Soon Cordelia fell asleep in her mother's lap, but Nat was too excited to feel sleepy.

Each told what had happened to them since their first master had died and the heirs sold off all the slaves. His mother had been fortunate because her new master had also purchased Nat's sister. Their new home had been on a small plantation on the peninsula, so when the Yankees invaded, it had been fairly easy to escape to Union lines.

Nat asked the question he knew had to be voiced even though he could guess the answer. "Do you know what happened to my brothers?"

Her voice broke in the darkness. "Never heard of any of

them again. Rufus will be thirteen now. Gabe is coming on ten, and Elihu is past eight. My poor, sweet children!" She reached over and clutched Nat's hand firmly. "I'm just mighty grateful to the Lord for letting me see you again, Nat. Mighty grateful."

Mother and son fell silent so that for about a full minute, the only sound was that of a log crumbling and falling into a campfire.

Finally, Nat cleared his throat. "Mama, I need to know: Who was my father? Is he still alive?"

"I don't know if he's alive or dead, but you must know a slave woman isn't allowed to name any white man who fathers one of her children."

"I've heard," Nat admitted, "but I had to ask."

His mother lowered her voice and leaned close to whisper in his ear. "You can't ever tell anyone, but it was the son of the white overseer at the Whitman plantation. Name was Travis. I was barely fifteen, and I didn't have any choice."

"I figured that." Nat paused, then murmured, "Travis. I think I'll call myself that: Nat Travis."

"I'm surprised. I thought you would hate it if you ever knew."

"Oh, I do in one way, but I want to remember why I hate it. A slave only has one name, and that's whatever the master decides it is. I'm not always going to be a slave, and I'll need two names."

"I know you'll be free someday, Nat. I know it in my heart, just as I know your sister and I will be free. So will my other children, even if I never see them again. I hear the soldiers talking about how Mr. Lincoln is going to free us all."

"He'll say it, Mama, but that won't make it so—not as long as the Confederacy holds out in this war. So I'm going to Richmond to see an abolitionist. I plan to make arrangements for you and Cordelia to be taken by the Underground Railroad to Canada. This man helped me escape there, so I'm sure he'll help you and Cord—"

★ ★

"You were free?" she interrupted in surprise. "Then why are you back here in the South?"

"I came to find you and Cordelia. Someday I hope to also find Rufus, Gabe, and Elihu."

His mother didn't say anything but suddenly bent and kissed him on the cheek. Her eyes were wet with tears.

"I have to go now," he said abruptly, hoping his voice didn't crack with his own deep emotions. "But I'll see you and Cordelia when we're all free."

He hurried off into the darkness, where his own tears quickly escaped and slid down his cheeks.

★  ★  ★  ★  ★

Gideon, Mrs. Tugwell, and John Fletcher sat on the front porch of the Tugwell home and made final plans for the risky trip to Richmond. They spoke in low tones so as not to awaken Ben, Kate, and Lilly.

Gideon said, "I remember what Emily wrote me about how William's body servant, Nat, escaped with a girl slave from Briarstone. Mr. Yates put some young peach trees on top of a false compartment at the bottom of his farm wagon, where he hid the runaways. I figure we can do the same with our wheat in case Yankee soldiers or our own troops stop us."

"I don't know," Fletcher mused. "A bumper crop of wheat is going to take up a lot more room than two hidden young people. In fact, having young trees riding high on your high-sided wagon might make foragers suspicious."

"Yes," Gideon replied, "but they would be much more likely to stop us if we drive along with just a piece of canvas thrown over the wheat."

"You've got a point," Fletcher admitted. "It's worth a try." He paused before adding, "I'm much more concerned about what might happen here while we're gone. Cobb was snooping around from the river, and you know how angry William got after you embarrassed him in the store."

★ ★

"We'll be all right," Mrs. Tugwell said.

"Just the same," Fletcher replied, "I think a word to William and Cobb might make them think twice about doing anything around here while we're gone."

"What do you mean, John?"

Gideon was surprised to hear his mother call Fletcher by his first name.

"I'd rather not say," he answered evasively. "Well, if you'll excuse me, I think I'll turn in."

After everyone said good-night and Fletcher walked toward his quarters in the barn, Gideon turned to his mother. "What do you think he's talking about, Mama?"

"I can only guess, but probably he's going to drop a warning to William and Cobb."

"You think that'll stop them?"

"I don't know, but if I were in their shoes, John Fletcher is one man I wouldn't want to cross."

Gideon looked up at the stars. He thought his mother was right, but would William and Cobb take that risk? Gideon was still thinking about that when he kissed his mother on the cheek and went inside to bed.

★ ★ ★ ★ ★

Emily's strong convictions gave her reassurance, so she was ready when Colonel Pemberton and his enlisted man returned. She stood and looked the tall officer in the eyes. "Sir, I have decided."

"Good!" he smiled approvingly and motioned to the other man to make notes. "Start from the beginning."

"First, I wish to speak to Mrs. Stonum, please."

A scowl replaced the smile. "Not until you've told me the truth."

"Very well." Her tone was polite but firm. "I have done nothing wrong. I am innocent of spying on the Confederacy." She sat down resolutely, defiantly crossing her arms across her chest. "That's the truth, and that's all I'll say until I talk to Mrs. Stonum."

Pemberton raised his voice in threat, but Emily met his gaze steadily and didn't say another word. After a few minutes, he grumbled, "You're a saucy one!"

Emily remained silent.

"Oh, all right!" Pemberton roared. "Let's go, but you'd better be ready to tell me what I want to know."

Standing, Emily promised, "I will tell you the gospel truth, sir, and nothing else." She followed him out the door. The enlisted man trailed after her.

★  ★  ★  ★  ★

Nat couldn't remember when he had been so happy as he picked his way among the Union tents amidst a chorus of heavy snores. He passed the last soldier's dying campfire and neared the darkened area where contraband men were quartered.

Suddenly, he sensed rather than heard something that made him spin around in alarm. Two forms rushed out of the darkness. By the faint glow of the distant campfire, he recognized Sergeant Kretzschmar swinging his pick handle. But before Nat could react, the club slammed into the side of his head. Bright flecks of light exploded before his eyes.

He dropped with a groan, dimly aware that a gag was being forced into his mouth and hand irons snapped on his wrists. Then the light flecks faded, and he slid into total blackness and silence.

★  ★  ★  ★  ★

Mrs. Stonum sat in her parlor, her face pale with concern. Hannah paced the floor and wailed in anguish after Emily and her two uniformed escorts finished telling what was going on.

"Oh, Emily!" Hannah cried, "I didn't mean for anything like this to happen! It's all my fault, and I'm so sorry!"

"I know." Knowing she was innocent made Emily calm.

★  ★

The widow motioned for Hannah to sit down, then turned to Emily, where she stood between the men. "I believe you, Emily," Mrs. Stonum said, "but you must convince these men that you're innocent of these awful charges. So tell them everything."

Emily took a deep breath, then explained. "I had promised not to tell, but Mr. Fitzhugh has falsely accused me. I no longer feel a burden of honor to keep the secret about our arrangement to carry my letters."

"Tell it from the beginning," Colonel Pemberton urged. "This man will take down what you say, and then you must sign it as a confession."

"I'll sign it as the truth," Emily declared, "and not as a confession, because I wasn't his accomplice."

"That's for the provost marshal's office to judge, Emily," Pemberton said. "Now, let's hear your side of this story."

Emily told about Fitzhugh's offer to carry her letters to and from Gideon. She gave Fitzhugh's reason for swearing her to secrecy. She concluded, "He said he wanted that news to share with others on his mail route. I thought it was a nice thing to do, so I agreed. But I never had any idea that he was going to use any of that information to spy against the Confederacy. And that's the truth, as God is my witness."

She closed her mouth, feeling emotionally drained, yet with a kind of peace.

Except for Hannah's quiet sniffling behind her handkerchief, there was a moment of silence before Mrs. Stonum spoke. "Gentlemen, I believe Emily, and so I will testify on her behalf if she goes to trial."

In her gratitude, Emily felt a gush of hot tears, but she blinked them back and turned to the colonel. She tried to read his reaction, but his face was a mask.

Barely breathing, Emily waited for his next words.

# THE SPY'S APPRENTICE

Late June rains and the heavy traffic of wheeled military vehicles and weapons turned the roads into deep mud. This delayed Gideon and Fletcher's uneventful entry into Richmond, where flour was expected to soon cost about sixteen dollars a barrel because of rampant inflation and increasing shortages. This pitted speculators against each other in bidding for the Tugwells' load of wheat. Gideon recalled last year when his father had insisted on gold instead of paper money in payment. The Confederacy never minted its own coins, so Fletcher and Gideon demanded twenty-five secretly hoarded U.S. twenty-dollar double eagles. Only one buyer could produce these, so the sale was made.

"Whoeee!" Gideon happily shouted when they drove the wagon beyond the speculator's hearing. "That five hundred dollars will not only pay the taxes by July first, but it will also give us cash for things we can't grow or make ourselves."

Fletcher looked around apprehensively. "If you don't want to risk being robbed by those plug-uglies I've read about in the *Richmond Examiner*, I wouldn't mention having any money."

"I forgot!" Gideon glanced down to where a false compartment under the high front seat served as a temporary hiding place for the gold coins.

"Well, time to decide," Fletcher declared. "Do we head for

home right now, or do we go see your friend while the roads dry up a little more?"

On the drive into the capital, with Hercules and a mule borrowed from Mr. Yates, Gideon had gone back and forth between the two choices. He had a keen desire to see Emily, but he also felt an urgent need to get home.

He asked, "Do you think William or Cobb dared do anything to the house or crops while we've been away?"

"Not if they're smart."

That was all Fletcher said, but Gideon knew what he meant. On the drive to Richmond, Fletcher had reluctantly told Gideon that he had personally spoken to both men. If there were any damaged crops, a fire, or even a threat to Mrs. Tugwell or the children, Fletcher would come looking for both William and Cobb. There had been no threat; just those few words, and William was smart. But Cobb wasn't.

Still, Gideon was comforted by the fact that on the morning he and Fletcher had left, Horatio came to the Tugwells' with some freedmen. They volunteered to look after things until Gideon and Fletcher returned.

Gideon reached into his pocket and produced a piece of paper. "Here's Emily's address on Franklin Street. Let's visit her for half an hour."

"Sounds good." Fletcher slapped the reins along the mules' backs. "Thirty minutes; then we head for home."

★ ★ ★ ★ ★

Nat's head still ached when the trader who had helped Sergeant Kretzschmar kidnap him drove into the heart of Richmond's old slave trade district. The rains had stopped and the sun shone brightly as Nat was led into a low, two-story brick house in the alley off of Wall Street, between Franklin and Main. Capitol Square was uphill about two blocks away.

A fifteen-foot-high brick wall with a massive wooden gate surrounded the house that served as a slave jail. The irons on

★ ★

Nat's legs and hands were removed in the courtyard. Several other prisoners looked at him without interest.

On the long ride through rain to the capital, Nat had almost driven himself into a frenzy because his mother and sister wouldn't know what had happened to him. They would vainly wait for a conductor from the Underground Railroad to spirit them out of the Union camp and into Canada.

Major Buckner would probably think Nat had run away, and Kretzschmar would naturally pretend to be totally ignorant of what had happened. Nat slowly came to realize that the sergeant's treachery would likely go unpunished. Nat accepted that. By the time he entered the jail, he had gained control of his emotions. His goal had not changed; he had to help his mother and sister escape to freedom. Dwelling on his circumstances wouldn't do that; using his brain would.

Careful to use slave dialect so he wouldn't make the other prisoners suspicious, he approached one with gray in his black hair and short, curly beard. "How long y'all bin heah?" Nat asked casually.

The man replied, "Jis' long 'nough to wash up, git us some decent food, an' into dese fine-lookin' clothes." He smiled, showing a gap between his two front teeth. "Dey gwine sell us so's we cain't he'p dig de fences round dis city. De mastahs don' want dem Yankees to set us free, so we's got to look good to dem buyers."

Under careful questioning, Nat learned that the "jail" was more like a boardinghouse, where slave traders fed the transient population for thirty cents a day. The place was not as depressing and grimy as other slave jails Nat had heard about.

He forced himself to walk away as though satisfied, but the older man followed him.

He lowered his voice. "Y'all got dat look."

"Look? What look is dat?"

"In yo'eyes. Oh, y'all don' need to put on no act wid me. I done lived long 'nough to see when one of us is a'thinkin' o'runnin' away. Well, I'm too old fo' dat, and I been whupped manys de time. But if'n I was yore age, an' knows what I does, I'd sho' find a way outta heah a'fore dey sell us. Got to be fast, 'cause dey don' hold public auctions; jist private-like. Next one gwine be in couple a hours."

"I don' know what y'all a'talkin' 'bout," Nat said.

"Yore eyes, dey say diff'rnt. Now if I'se r'aht, y'all soon 'nough be over by de cou't ya'd gate."

The old man didn't point, but Nat followed his eyes. The sturdy wooden gate was reinforced with a heavy iron Z-shaped brace. "What is dey pas't dat?" Nat asked.

"*Free*dom! Dat's what. Sweet *free*dom fo' a boy wid long legs what kin run fast."

After the man walked away, Nat forced himself to wait until he was the only one in the courtyard. Then he looked around before casually sauntering around the high brick fence toward the gate. He kept moving while his eyes desperately probed for any unusual flaw. Even so, he almost missed it.

The lower metal bolt in the right hinge had about half an inch sticking up. It was shiny instead of rusted like the top bolt. Nat walked on by, frowning. Then he understood what that meant. Some prisoner had worked the lower bolt loose so that if it was pulled, the gate would sag slightly. Pushed aside, there would likely be enough room for a slender person to slip through.

Nat thought of waiting for darkness but remembered that the private sale would begin in less than two hours. He quickly probed the empty courtyard to make sure no one was watching. Satisfied, he walked back to the gate. He grasped the bolt and pulled. It was tight, but the rust had been broken free, so it came out fairly easily. The gate sagged, allowing Nat to see the alley.

Nat didn't even look back but threw himself on the ground and slid through the opening. He jumped up and took a quick look around. The nearest cross street beckoned to his left. He turned that direction and raced away.

A man shouted behind him, and Nat recognized the slave trader's voice. At the first corner, he turned right and ran hard toward Franklin Street.

★  ★  ★  ★  ★

Mrs. Stonum had convinced the provost marshal's officer that a Richmond cell was no place for a thirteen-year-old girl. On her honor, Emily was placed under house arrest and the hand irons were removed. She was remanded to the custody of Mrs. Stonum on the condition that she could not leave the house on Franklin Street until her trial.

Day after day, Emily was alone in the quiet house. The widow left each morning to do volunteer nursing at the hospital. Hannah, still contrite over her part in getting Emily arrested, went to work at the arsenal.

Besides the danger of possibly being hanged as a spy, Emily fretted about Brice and his wounded arm. To help pass the time and to work off her emotions, she cleaned out and rearranged the cupboards and pantry. Every piece of furniture was polished before she scrubbed all the downstairs hardwood floors on her hands and knees.

She had started on the second-story floors when there was a knock at the front door. Eager to talk to someone, no matter who, she hurried downstairs.

She opened the door to see a haggard woman with a baby cradled in her left arm and a tattered carpetbag in her right hand. Two small children clung to her skirts. It was a familiar sight to Emily; day after day, displaced women and children came to Mrs. Stonum's door. So Emily knew what the woman wanted before she spoke.

"Good morning, miss. I heard you folks have rooms to rent. Have you got one for me and my babies?"

Emily's heart went out to the mother and her children. "I'm sorry, but every room is taken."

★  ★

The woman sighed. "That's what I hear everywhere I go. Hotels, boardinghouses, private homes. Can't even find one room. Well, thank you kindly anyway."

Emily watched the homeless family slowly walk away. *This terrible war!* she thought bitterly. *Everybody has troubles, yet I can't help. I can't even help myself!*

She went back upstairs to her scrubbing, but her heart ached for the woman and all those like her trying to find a place to sleep in a city where the enemy was so close.

★ ★ ★ ★ ★

From his high seat in the empty wagon, Gideon told Fletcher, "We should be getting close. Emily said her place was near the capitol. I see that up on the hill."

"I'm glad we got off of Main Street," the man replied. "Seems like everyone in Virginia is either trying to get into Richmond or out of it."

"Seems like," Gideon agreed. "But from what the grain speculators said, it must have been really awful right after the battle at the end of last month and first of this. That must have been some sight, with rich and poor, black and white, bringing food or water to the wounded while they waited to get into a hospital or see a surgeon."

Gideon's eyes were drawn to a youth running toward them in the street. Pointing, Gideon said, "He had better look out! He almost got hit by that dray wagon, but he didn't even slow—" Gideon broke off his sentence and stared.

"What's the matter?" Fletcher asked.

"That looks like Nat from Briarstone."

"The one who taught you to read in a pit school?"

"Yes!" Gideon stood up to see better. "That's who it is! Emily wrote me that Nat had escaped to Canada by the Underground Railroad, so what's he doing here?"

"The way he's looking over his shoulder, I'd say that somebody is chasing him."

★ ★

"You're probably right. Please pull over!"

Fletcher brought the team to a halt just as Nat neared, dodging pedestrian, horse, and carriage traffic in his wild flight.

"Nat!" Gideon called through cupped hands. "Nat!"

For the first time, the fugitive glanced up, did a double take, then swerved toward the empty wagon. "I ran away, but they're after me!" he called.

"Jump in the wagon!" Gideon cried. "Crouch down out of sight!"

"Thanks!" Nat leaped up on the wagon spokes, grabbed the high sides with both hands, and threw himself over the top. He scrambled underneath the canvas that had been used to hide the wheat.

"Let's get out of here!" Gideon exclaimed, turning back to Fletcher.

"We're going!" he answered and slapped the lines sharply against the team's backs.

Gideon twisted in the seat to look behind. A couple of women stared after the wagon, but there didn't seem to be anyone running after Nat.

"Now what?" Fletcher asked under his breath as the team broke into a slow trot. "Somebody might soon be looking for this wagon."

Gideon hesitated. He was surely within a few blocks of Emily's house. But should he risk going on to see her? Or would it be wiser to head out of town?

"Well?" Fletcher prompted.

"Emily knows Nat from when they both lived at Briarstone. She'll want to see him. So let's go there, but we'll only stay a few minutes."

"Then look sharp for that address, Gideon. We've got a wagonload of trouble, but from what you told me about the way William treated Nat, we've got to help him."

★ ★

★ ★ ★ ★ ★

Emily was still scrubbing the second-story hardwood floor when someone pounded loudly on the front door. She hurried downstairs expecting another desperate fugitive family seeking lodging. She opened the door and gasped. "Gideon! And Nat!"

Gideon started to say they could only stay a few minutes, but instead, he blurted in surprise, "You've grown up!" Instantly embarrassed, he stammered, "Uh . . . I mean . . ."

"You've changed, too," she replied quickly, helping cover his embarrassment. Her smile indicated she liked the change. She motioned them inside, closed the door, then turned to Nat. "I thought you were in Canada."

"I was, but it's a long story." He stepped to the nearest window to cautiously peer out.

"Is someone chasing you?" she asked anxiously.

"Yes. I just escaped from a slave jail minutes ago."

Gideon added, "He was running down the street when we picked him up, so we can only stay a few minutes."

Her face clouded. "Oh . . ." she said in a small voice.

"Something wrong?" Gideon asked.

"My story is like Nat's," she replied with a controlled sigh of disappointment. "A long one." She looked up at the man. "You must be John Fletcher. Gideon wrote me about you."

"And you're Emily Lodge," he replied with a warm grin. "Now I can see why Gideon speaks so highly of you."

Emily felt her face suddenly turn very warm. "I am so glad to see all of you!" she exclaimed, sweeping each with an affectionate glance. "Gideon, I want to hear all about what's happened since your last letter. And, Nat, I'm dying to know why you left Canada."

"You first, Emily," Gideon prompted. "Tell us what you've been doing. I haven't seen Fitzhugh for a long time, so I don't know if you've written—" He stopped abruptly when she closed her eyes and flinched as though in pain. "What is it? Has he quit delivering our mail?"

"He's going to be hanged for treason!" Emily exclaimed. "And he got me arrested for helping him!"

"What?" Gideon exclaimed.

"You were arrested?" Nat added.

"I am still under house arrest!" she replied, fighting hard to control the fierce emotions that seized her. "I can't even leave here to try getting Fitzhugh to tell the truth and clear my name! They're threatening to hang me, too!"

Gideon's mouth dropped open. He stood dumbfounded, staring, unable to believe her words.

Fletcher said quietly, "Nat, you can see we can't leave her right now, but those slave traders will be looking for you. Do you want to go off on your own or take a chance and stay here until we can help you leave?"

"I don't think they would look for me here. Besides, Emily helped me escape from Briarstone. I'll stay."

Emily flashed him a grateful smile, but tears glistened on her eyelashes. "Thank you, Nat."

Gideon spoke up again. "Tell us how this happened, Emily."

★ ★

# RACING THE GALLOWS

Emily briefly told everything, from Fitzhugh's offer to deliver her letters to the arrest. She finished by saying, "I don't blame Hannah. She didn't know that what she said to the provost marshal would lead them to Fitzhugh, or that he would say I helped him. Everything he ever said made me believe he was loyal to the South. I never dreamed that he was a Union spy, but he certainly knows I'm not."

"Why would he do such an awful thing?" Gideon asked.

"I don't know, but the only time he let Mrs. Stonum talk to him, he said he was mad at Hannah for getting him caught. So Mrs. Stonum thinks he's taking his anger out on me because he can't touch Hannah. Oh, this whole thing is so terrible, and I can't do a thing to save myself!"

Gideon was deeply moved with anger toward Fitzhugh and compassion for Emily. He reached out and gently touched her arm. "You said Fitzhugh won't even talk to Mrs. Stonum, but maybe he'll let me see him."

Emily's face lit up with hope. "You think so?"

"I'll go try," Gideon assured her.

Fletcher said, "I'll go with you. Where is he?"

"Libby Prison," she replied. "It's down by the river—on Cary, between Eighteenth and Nineteenth Streets."

"We'll find it," Gideon declared. He turned to Nat. "What do you want to do right now?"

"Well, I can't risk having the traders find me here and maybe get Emily into more trouble. If I could borrow some different clothes and a hat, I could probably safely go see the man who helped me escape to Canada."

Emily volunteered, "Mrs. Stonum still has a closetful of her husband's clothes. She told me she's going to give them away. Maybe—"

"They'll have to do," Nat interrupted.

"I'll show you where they are." Emily turned to Gideon and Fletcher. "I'll pray for all three of you."

Gideon nodded but didn't trust himself to speak. He headed out the door, overwhelmed at the realization that this was Emily's last hope.

★ ★ ★ ★ ★

Guiding the mules toward the James River, Gideon asked in a hoarse voice that threatened to break, "What if Fitzhugh won't let us talk to him?"

"He'll do it, one way or another," the man replied grimly. "But if it'll ease your mind any, I don't think the Confederacy would hang a young girl. We're not that kind of people."

Gideon brightened, then frowned. "But she can't spend her life in prison, either. She would never get home to see her friend Jessie or live a normal life. We've got to get Fitzhugh to tell the truth somehow!"

"We'll do it, Gideon. Trust in God to help us say or do the right things to make Fitzhugh clear her."

Gideon nodded but didn't speak. He was aware that although Fletcher had gone to church with the family, this was the first time he had made a clear reference to his personal faith.

"You mentioned her best friend in Illinois," Fletcher said. "I noticed that when Emily told about helping Brice in the hospital, and Hannah telling the provost marshal about him, that you got a strange look on your face. Don't you like Brice?"

"It's not that." Gideon didn't know how to explain that he didn't want any other boy to notice Emily. He remembered how upset he had been about a year ago when she had asked him to mail a letter to Brice. He had also been very upset when he had learned that Brice had told Emily he was going to marry her when she grew up. Gideon didn't then realize why such things upset him. Now he knew. He liked Emily very much. Never before had he experienced any emotion like that about a girl.

"She's very pretty," Fletcher commented. "She's going to grow up to be a beautiful young woman."

Gideon surprised himself by snapping, "I don't want to talk about it! Can't you make those mules go any faster?"

Fletcher called to the mules and flicked the reins against their backs. As they picked up speed, Gideon thought he saw a faint smile on the driver's face.

★ ★ ★ ★ ★

After Gideon and Fletcher left the house, Nat changed into clothes and a hat that had belonged to the widow's late husband. At the front door, he paused. "What do you think, Miss Emily? Will I be recognized?"

"Please just call me Emily, and I think you look like a young white man wearing clothes that don't quite fit."

"Thanks . . . Emily," he replied, although it was against his training to address a white girl in such an informal manner. He added, "I trust you because you and Mr. Yates helped Sarah and me escape from Briarstone. Now I must—"

"Sarah!" Emily broke in, trying to keep her mind off of Gideon and Fletcher's fearsome mission. "She did a brave thing for you when my cousin William whipped you before you both ran away. How is she?"

"I haven't seen her since we got to Richmond back then." He paused, aware that even thinking of Sarah gave him a warm feeling. He wished he could see her again, but slaves didn't dare have many wishes. "Anyway," he added, "I must find a man named Edward Reverdy."

"Oh, I know who you mean. He's an abolitionist, like Mr. Yates. Of course, I don't know of anyone around here besides me who knows that about either of them—even Mrs. Stonum—although some people suspect they are. Mr. Reverdy has an office in back of a tobacco warehouse on the riverfront. I can give you directions."

Moments later, Nat stepped outside and glanced around to make sure no suspicious-looking people were in sight. Then he boldly walked toward the waterfront.

★ ★ ★ ★ ★

The house seemed more quiet and lonely than ever after everyone was gone, and Emily was alone with her thoughts. She returned to her scrub brush and pail, vigorously completing the upstairs floors while she silently prayed for Gideon and Fletcher to succeed in their mission, and for Nat to escape the slave traders who were searching for him.

She was startled to hear the front door open. Emily frowned. *Who could that be? It's too early for either Mrs. Stonum or Hannah to come home.*

Brushing long golden curls away from her face, Emily stood up and called, "Who's there?"

"It's me," the widow replied.

Emily rushed to the top of the stairs. "Why're you home so—? Oh! What happened to your arm?"

"I broke it tripping over a broom at the hospital."

Taking the stairs two at a time, Emily reached the ground floor and approached Mrs. Stonum, whose right arm was in a sling. "How bad is it?" she asked.

"A simple fracture, the surgeon said, but I can't nurse anyone because of it."

"Oh, I'm so sorry, Mrs. Stonum! Is there anything I can do for you?"

"No, thanks. It'll just take time to heal. Well, on second thought, I've got a little tea left. Would you make a pot? I have something else to talk to you about."

Emily wanted to tell about Gideon and Nat, but the widow's grave expression alerted Emily to the fact that now was not the best time. "Oh?" she prompted, heading toward the kitchen, the widow following.

"Before I went to work at the hospital this morning, I tried to see President Davis in hopes he would grant you clemency, but he wasn't available."

Emily used the long-handled dipper to ladle water from a bucket into the metal tea kettle. "I hadn't thought of that, but thanks for trying."

Mrs. Stonum sat down at the table. "There's more."

An ominous note in the woman's voice made Emily turn to look sharply at her. *More bad news!*

"I went by to visit your friend Brice, as you asked, and told him what was going on."

"Is he all right?"

"He was in good spirits, like all those brave boys. You know, I never cease to marvel at how they stay so cheerful even when they're suffering so terribly."

Emily sensed that Mrs. Stonum was suddenly talking too fast, almost babbling, as though avoiding saying something else unpleasant. "His arm," Emily started to ask, feeling a prickle of alarm. "Can it be saved?"

The woman closed her eyes and lowered her head.

"No!" Emily cried, almost dropping the teacups she had taken from the cupboard. "He can't lose it!"

Opening her eyes, Mrs. Stonum whispered, "The surgeons say it's either amputate or he'll die."

Emily sagged weakly into a chair. "Oh no! Oh no!" She remembered caring for a Confederate teen from Georgia whose leg had been amputated after he suffered a Minié ball wound. He had told her that he knew he was going to die because those

★ ★

who had arms or legs cut off usually did.

Emily had tried to reassure him that it wasn't true. She had been around the wounded long enough to hear that surgeons commonly amputated arms and legs. Many patients did die, but not all. Emily tried to comfort the soldier. Two days later, he was dead.

Mrs. Stonum said, "I'm sorry to keep hitting you with such bad news, but you'd find out sooner or later."

Emily shook her head, whispering, "Not Brice!"

"There's one more thing you need to hear."

Emily groaned. "Isn't this enough already?"

"It is, my dear, but I've got to tell you."

Emily gripped the edge of the table with both hands and waited, her mouth dry, her pulse racing.

"During the noon mealtime," Mrs. Stonum continued in a sad voice, "I tried again to see Fitzhugh, but he wouldn't talk to me this time, either."

Emily wasn't surprised, but she swallowed hard, afraid that Gideon and Fletcher would fail, too. "I am grateful for your efforts," she said sincerely. "Now I have some news—"

"They've moved up the execution date!" the widow interrupted with a catch in her voice.

Emily jerked as if she had been slapped. "What?"

"The officials are afraid the Yankees still might take the city, despite General Jackson and General Lee's ongoing counteroffensive. They want to be sure that Fitzhugh is executed before that happens. It'll be today."

"Today! What time?" Emily asked in a hoarse whisper.

"They were getting ready when I left the prison."

Emily's thoughts flashed to Gideon and Fletcher, now on their way to the prison. *Are they already too late?*

★　★　★　★　★

Following Emily's directions, Nat soon heard the sounds of boats on the James River and smelled the stored tobacco near

★　★

the waterfront. Memories flowed back to that night when he and Sarah were lowered through a trap door in a small back room of such a warehouse.

*Two rowboats without lanterns rocked below. A rope ladder was lowered and Sarah backed down in the darkness, guided by a silent crewman. She stretched out in the bottom of one boat. Nat was wordlessly conducted into the second boat. In the faint glow of reflected shore lamps, he made out a piece of canvas being placed over Sarah. It was the last he saw of her before he was similarly covered in the other boat. The first leg of the long Atlantic journey to Canada began.*

Nat sighed heavily, took a deep breath, and entered the side door to the warehouse. He headed toward a small sign over a door: Edward Reverdy, Buyer.

★　★　★　★　★

Libby Prison had been a warehouse before it was turned into a military prison for captured Union troops. Gideon's eyes swept the long, three-story structure with twin brick chimneys sticking up above both ends of the roof. Prisoners stared out of the twenty windows on each floor. There was one pole gas lamp on the dirt street, and a few white tents were pitched in front. Otherwise, the place was plain and barren.

Although mostly Union officers were confined here, the city was so short of space for captured prisoners that the civilian, Oliver Fitzhugh, had been held here for his high crime of treason.

Gideon noticed a Confederate soldier open a gate to a high-walled courtyard on the side of the prison. At the far end, he gulped at the sight of a waiting gallows. He glanced at Fletcher and realized he had also seen the ghastly structure, but neither mentioned it.

Silently intent on their urgent mission, they left the team and wagon and started toward the nearest door. It opened, and a small procession of men walked out led by two Confederate

★　★

soldiers with bayonets fixed to their rifles. Behind them came two men in civilian clothes. The one wearing a dark suit carried a Bible. He walked beside a slender man in his thirties. A couple of other uniformed officers wearing blue kepis were next, while four more riflemen brought up the rear. They were escort guards to accompany the condemned man to his execution and prevent any possible rescue attempt.

Gideon grabbed Fletcher's arm. "That's Fitzhugh by the man with the Bible! I've seen him at Church Creek!"

"Come on!" Fletcher exclaimed and hurried toward the little procession.

The riflemen immediately pointed their weapons toward the approaching man and boy. The taller of the officers called out, "Halt! Stay where you are!"

Gideon and Fletcher stopped dead still, but Gideon called, "We must speak to Mr. Fitzhugh!"

The officer replied, "It's too late, so leave."

Gideon cried in an anguished voice, "We can't! He knows that Emily Lodge is no spy! He's got to clear her name." He turned imploring eyes on the prisoner. "Please! Tell the truth!"

Fitzhugh looked at him without interest, making the boy's hopes plummet.

"I'm Colonel Pemberton," the tall officer said. "Who're you?"

"I'm Gideon Tugwell, Emily's friend from Church Creek. He's John Fletcher. Please, mister . . ." Gideon's voice cracked as he struggled with a hopeless situation.

Fletcher said, "Begging your pardon, Colonel, but I'm sure you don't want an innocent girl to die when your prisoner can prove her innocence."

Pemberton's eyes dropped to Fletcher's missing left hand. "Where did you serve, Fletcher?"

"Manassas, sir. If we could have a few minutes with your prisoner . . ." He left the sentence dangling.

Pemberton turned to Fitzhugh. "You want to talk, or finish

★ ★

our walk?" He jerked his head toward the gallows.

As the condemned man hesitated, Gideon blinked back tears of desperation that blurred his vision. "Please!"

The colonel said, "Fitzhugh, I believe that girl is innocent, but I can't prove it. You can, but only you."

The prisoner shrugged but didn't speak.

Gideon exclaimed, "Do you want to stand before your Maker knowing that you had a last chance to save Emily when you know she's not guilty?"

Fitzhugh didn't speak or move.

Colonel Pemberton sighed heavily. "All right, men. Let's finish the job."

Gideon gave a strangled cry and turned away, tears scalding down his cheeks. He heard the soldiers shoulder their rifles.

"Wait!" Fitzhugh's voice made the boy whirl around. He was barely able to see through misted eyes, but Gideon heard the prisoner ask, "Anybody got a pencil?"

# WHISTLING DIXIE

Nat had only seen Edward Reverdy briefly by lantern light, so he didn't remember much about him. In daylight, having told the abolitionist of his goal to have his mother and sister spirited to freedom, the boy had a moment to study the man sitting across the desk from him.

His short stature and slight build didn't match Nat's idea of an Underground Railroad conductor who dared take great risks to help slaves escape to Canada. His dark eyes squinted through wire-rimmed spectacles.

"Very well," he told Nat. "I'll do what I can to get them to freedom. But what about you?"

Nat admitted, "I have mixed feelings. I'd like to be free and not keep worrying about being caught to either be sold back into bondage or returned to William Lodge. But I'm also hoping to locate my three brothers."

"That's commendable but unrealistic," Reverdy said bluntly. "Most separated slave families never see any of their relatives again."

"I know, but my mother always said that 'winning is in the mind,' and I keep thinking I can find my brothers."

"It's dangerous for us to be together long, so let's cut this short. If you want to return to Canada, be here tomorrow night about midnight. Don't let anyone see you."

"I'll be careful, but if I don't show up, you'll know why.

Thanks for helping my mother and sister."

★　★　★　★　★

Emily kept watching out of the front window for Gideon and Fletcher to return, but she didn't expect to see Hannah arrive in a hackney. Aware that her roommate's twelve-and-a-half-cents-an-hour job required a twelve-hour shift, Emily knew that only something very important would let Hannah quit early. It was also very expensive for Hannah to hire a hack.

Emily raised her voice so Mrs. Stonum could hear her upstairs. "Hannah's home! Something must be wrong!"

"I'll be right down," the widow called as Emily hurried from the window to open the door for Hannah.

"Are you all right?" Emily asked anxiously.

Hannah grinned. "I'm better, thanks."

"What happened?" Emily asked, hearing Mrs. Stonum rapidly decending the stairs.

Hannah threw her arms around Emily. "Oh, I've been eating my heart out since I got you in trouble because of what I told those men from the provost marshal's office."

Emily was confused. Hannah had grinned at her upon entering the house, but now her body started to shake as if she were suddenly weeping.

Hannah's voice broke as she continued. "I was so upset at work that my supervisor was afraid I'd do something wrong and blow up the place. He told me to go home early. He even paid for the hack."

"I've told you to stop blaming yourself," Emily protested, drawing back so she could see her roommate's eyes bright with anguished tears.

"Yes," Mrs. Stonum said, "Emily's right, Hannah. You asked her forgiveness and she gave it. We both know you didn't mean to do Emily any harm."

"I know, but . . ." Hannah released Emily and brushed a tear from her cheek. "But if anything happens to you, Emily,

★　★

I'd die of shame, so I wanted to do something for you. I didn't have enough for a gift, but . . ."

When Hannah didn't finish her sentence, Emily said, "You don't need to get me anything. Besides, I have faith that this will all work out somehow."

"You're so brave," Hannah exclaimed, "but I had to do something or I'd lose my mind. So I took some of my own money to put with what the supervisor gave. First, I took the hack to see the provost marshal, but he wasn't in. Then I stopped by the hospital to ask your friend if I could do something for him since you couldn't."

"Oh dear!" Mrs. Stonum cried. "Then you must know what the surgeons were planning to do!"

"Yes. Brice told me. While I was trying to comfort him, the sergeant who is the surgeon's assistant came in. Brice said to me, 'I guess this is where I lose my arm.' But instead, the steward went to the patient next to him, took a bandage off him, and put it on a third man."

Emily grimaced, knowing that a shortage of bandages meant some had to be reused on other patients. But she was anxious about Hannah's long-winded report. "Please!" Emily interrupted. "What're you trying to say?"

"I'm coming to that! When Brice asked the steward when they were going to come for him, he said, 'After the surgeon last examined you, he told me your arm is looking better. It may not have to be amputated!'"

★ ★ ★ ★ ★

Following his short meeting with Reverdy, Nat felt that he was lucky to have found his mother and sister. But the abolitionist was right. It was very unlikely that Nat could find his brothers. The logical thing for him to do was to return tonight and be helped back to Canada.

Crossing Main on his way up to Franklin Street, Nat saw a stopped coffle. About two dozen barefoot slaves sat in a line

★ ★

along the coffle chain, which linked them to each other. There were men, women, and children, all with chains circling their waists. Their wrists were manacled with iron cuffs. They sat in resignation, without hope, resting their chains on the ground.

Suddenly, Nat froze at the sight of the same slave trader who had captured him after he was assaulted by Sergeant Kretzschmar. The trader was talking to a couple of white mounted drovers with pistols and whips, who were obviously in charge of the coffle.

A voice beside Nat made him jump. "Seeing a sight like that makes you glad you're not black, doesn't it?"

Nat instinctively started to run, then remembered his borrowed clothes. He nodded, turning his head so that the borrowed hat hid his curly hair and face from the stocky white man. He wore a wide hat favored by planters.

The stranger mused, "Sometimes it almost makes a man feel sorry for them. I see them go through here all the time. Some owner sells a bunch of field hands, and those drovers make them walk as far as Georgia. Once a drover told me that only takes six weeks. 'Course, the drovers ride horseback and use their whips a bit."

Nat didn't want the man to look at him closely, so Nat pointed. "Do those little ones make it all right?"

"Not all of them. Sometimes they get left by the roadside. But even those who get there won't live more than a few years. Heat, disease, and hard work make them die young."

Nat skimmed the coffle, noting that one boy facing away was about the age of his brother, Rufus, who was thirteen.

The planter continued. "But judging from the way the drovers are talking to the slave trader, tonight this gang won't have to sleep on the hard ground. Not that the slave jail is much more comfortable, but at least it's got a roof in case it rains. Well, I've got to be going."

As the man walked away, Nat started to turn to continue toward the Stonum house. At that moment, the boy whose

* *

back had been toward him turned around. Nat was so startled he exclaimed aloud, "Rufus!"

★ ★ ★ ★ ★

Emily was encouraged by Hannah's report that Brice might not lose his arm, but she still waited by the front window for Gideon and Fletcher to return. Her life hung on the success of their mission.

Finally, her vigil paid off. She saw the team and wagon pulling to the curb in front of the house. "They're here!" she cried and ran out the door, fear and faith struggling so violently inside her mind that she could barely breathe.

She looked at their faces, trying to guess if their desperate mission had succeeded. She couldn't tell as Gideon jumped down from the seat while Fletcher wrapped the reins around the brake handle.

Gideon ran toward her, holding up a piece of paper. "We got it, Emily! A signed confession! You're clear!"

A joyous scream burst from her lips. "Oh, thank God! Thank you, too! And Mr. Fletcher." She rushed to meet Gideon, her eyes on the paper. "Let me see! Let me see!"

His grin was so wide his face felt as if it might split, but he didn't care as he handed her the paper. "It's like a deathbed confession," he told her, his voice sobering. "Written and signed by Fitzhugh and witnessed by the colonel and the preacher walking with him. You're cleared, Emily! You're going free!"

"Oh, Gideon!" She looked up from the document and impulsively threw her arms around him. "Thank you so much!"

He stiffened in surprise, feeling the soft brush of her long blond hair against his cheek. Then she released him and did the same to Fletcher, all the time bubbling with happy words while her voice kept breaking so she couldn't be understood.

Until now, Mrs. Stonum had quietly remained in the back-

★ ★

ground. She cleared her throat. "I want to add my congratulations to all of you, and to ask if Emily can stand one more piece of good news without bursting?"

Everyone turned to Emily, who checked her joyous babbling to ask, "What is it?"

"Well," the widow began, "I had been thinking about what I could do while my broken arm healed. I am now confident that the colonel will expedite your pass, and I'm sure one could be issued to me so that I could accompany you to—"

"Oh, Mrs. Stonum!" Emily interrupted with a jubilant shriek. "Thank you!" She rushed to the widow and threw both arms around her neck, so overcome she could not speak but could only make happy sounds. Words weren't necessary, for everyone knew it was a time for joyous noises.

★  ★  ★  ★  ★

On the way back to the Tugwell farm, Gideon still radiated with an inner warmth he had never known before. It wasn't just that he and Fletcher had helped save Emily from possible execution. Part of his glow was the memory of her impulsive hug and her hair brushing his cheek.

Fletcher observed with a little smile, "I think I'm seeing a boy who's becoming a man."

"Huh?" Gideon asked absently. "Oh," he added, understanding that he was being teased. "I was just thinking about . . . everything—the way it turned out."

"Couldn't have been better," Fletcher agreed, driving the team with his one hand. "You and your mother will not only be able to pay off the taxes but also have enough to carry you through the winter."

"It couldn't have been done without you," Gideon answered soberly.

"I'm glad I could help."

"When we get home," Gideon said, "I'm going back to my father's grave. Before you showed up that day, I was so mis-

★ ★

erable I said some wrong things about my father. I know he can't hear me, but I want to say I'm sorry."

"I understand, and I'm sure he would, too."

"I wish he could really be here. Anyway, I'm glad my mother won't have to marry Cobb to save our farm."

"Your mother is a very fine woman."

Gideon glanced at Fletcher, wondering if he was becoming interested in her. Then he remembered that after the fall harvest, Fletcher planned to move on.

That saddened Gideon, so he shifted his thoughts to what had been said about expediting Emily's pass. Mrs. Stonum would easily get hers, and Emily would finally be on her way home—unless something unexpected happened.

Gideon forced that thought away. He told Fletcher, "By then, she'll be able to tell her friend Jessie if her brother's arm was saved. He'll be a prisoner of war until this thing finally ends. But Nat and other slaves won't ever really be free."

"From what I hear, Lincoln thinks differently," Fletcher commented.

"It'll take more than words to free them. Anyway, I'm glad we were still at the house when Nat reported seeing his brother. I admire Nat for deciding to try freeing him."

Fletcher said, "I hope he does, too, although I never heard of anyone escaping from a coffle."

"Nat is a very determined person. So's Emily."

"I got that impression from both of them."

Gideon said, "I'm going to write Emily and tell her what I didn't get a chance to tell her this trip. After knowing Nat, and the way Horatio and his friends came to help us at the farm, I can see how God made all people of the same blood."

"So can I. But have you made up your mind how you feel about slavery?"

"I'm still struggling with that." Gideon glanced back, glad to see that Richmond still stood as the capital of the Confederacy. It would be great news to share with his family. He hoped

★ ★

that William and Cobb didn't have some unpleasant surprise waiting for him. Even if they did, Gideon was anxious to get home with the money his mother so desperately needed.

"Can't you make these mules go faster?" he asked.

"No," Fletcher said with a smile, "but maybe if you whistled a happy tune, it might help pass the time."

Gideon grinned. "I'll whistle fast, and maybe the team will go faster, too." He puckered up and began sprightly whistling "Dixie."

# EPILOGUE

*October 17, 1933*

In June and early July of 1862, nearly seventy years ago, we in the South thought we had witnessed a near miracle after two major battles fought outside of Richmond.

Emily was there when General Joe Johnston was severely wounded on May 31 at the Battle of Seven Pines (Fair Oaks). He was replaced by General Robert E. Lee.

Emily, Nat, and I were there when Yankee invaders were within sight of Richmond's church steeples. While we three were fighting our own personal battles, badly outnumbered Lee and General "Stonewall" Jackson boldly attacked the Union's General George McClellan from June 25 to July 1. The vast Federal army retreated down the peninsula.

Richmond, capital and heart of the Confederacy, was saved even though Lee technically did not win any of the battles in what is now called the Seven Days Campaign.

Out of those hard days, Emily's *honesty* helped clear her name. Nat's *determination* started his mother and sister on their way from slavery to freedom. And I found the *courage* to do what had to be done in spite of the obstacles.

However, the war was not over, and neither were troubles for Emily, Nat, and me.

Emily expected to head for her home in Illinois, but a major surprise waited for her.

Nat knew he was setting out on a difficult mission, but he had no idea of the unexpected twist of fate ahead.

And while I was happily whistling on the way home from Richmond, it was soon time for a different tune.

I'll tell you about all of that, and what happened next in the war, when again I open the pages of my boyhood journal.

# Early Teen Fiction Series From Bethany House Publishers
### (Ages 11–14)

———— ⊷⊶⊷ ————

BETWEEN TWO FLAGS • by Lee Roddy
Join Gideon, Emily, and Nat as they face the struggles of growing up during the Civil War.

THE ALLISON CHRONICLES • by Melody Carlson
Follow along as Allison O'Brian, the daughter of a famous 1940s movie star, searches for the truth about her past and the love of a family.

HIGH HURDLES • by Lauraine Snelling
Show jumper DJ Randall strives to defy the odds and achieve her dream of winning Olympic Gold.

SUMMERHILL SECRETS • by Beverly Lewis
Fun-loving Merry Hanson encounters mystery and excitement in Pennsylvania's Amish country.

THE TIME NAVIGATORS • by Gilbert Morris
Travel back in time with Danny and Dixie as they explore unforgettable moments in history.